FREE INDEED

FREE INDEED

A NOVEL

Rev. Brian C. Johnson, PhD

WordCrafts Press

Free Indeed
Copyright © 2025
Brian C. Johnson, PhD

Hardback ISBN: 978-1-962218-99-3
Paperback ISBN: 978-1-967649-00-6

Cover concept and design by Mike Parker.

Published by WordCrafts Press
Cody, Wyoming 82414
www.wordcrafts.net

To the memory of Bishop Allen.
A true giant of black history regrettably forgotten.
I'm honored to be a recipient of your gift to the world.

Chapter 1

Down by the Riverside

A voice from the heavens declared, 'This is my beloved Son, hear ye him.'" Pastor Richard Allen wiped sweat from his brow with a worn-out kerchief as he preached on an early, hot August day to the black congregation of Lovely Lane Chapel where they gathered in the common area outside the church. "I believe that day I heard God's call to preach his word. From my own baptism day, I committed myself to telling the truth about the God-awful thing called slavery. Although it was my master who had allowed me to attend the Methodist revival services going on, I emerged from the water and cried unto him who delighted to hear the prayers of a poor sinner. Suddenly, my dungeon shook, my chains fell off, and 'Glory to God,' I cried. My soul was filled. I was free!"

A woman in a dark blue dress stood and yelled, "Praise the Lord!"

Allen smiled as others joined in her cry. His message of Jesus' baptism connected to his own, and his people understood.

As he dismissed the congregation, he said, "Be free, y'all. Live in freedom this week."

Allen stood near the front of the church a few moments later, greeting the remaining stragglers. He noticed the Hubbards waiting for him at the rear of the church. He shook the last congregant's hand and approached the Hubbard family with a humble smile.

"Good word today, Pastor," Brother Hubbard gushed. "I'll be chewing on that one for a while.' I need to read that passage more deeply."

"Thank you, Brother. That is always my goal as a preacher—to encourage others to study further." Allen motioned for them to move to the shade of a large oak tree. "I don't want people to just take my messages at face value. I want them to accept it because they understand for themselves. That's why everything I teach is the word of God and not my opinion."

Allen let the breeze blow through his sweat-drenched shirt a moment before asking, "Which part did you connect with?"

Lenny Hubbard stood with his hat in his hand. "I like how you made it real for us. I could remember playing in the water like that when I was a kid, but you made the baptism come to life for me. I was transported. Honey, what would you say?"

"Oh, I don't know. It was good though."

Sister Hubbard's attention was drawn away to where the Hubbard's house stood across the square. Allen knew she was probably wondering if the space had been adequately prepared for 'his presence for lunch."

"We better put some pep in our steps," she said. "Looks like it's going to rain."

If she was anything like Allen's wife, she was more worried about the potential of muddy footprints on her freshly mopped floors. He watched as she harangued her children. Her young son attempted to run away from her, but she tightened her grip.

"Now, hold my hand, Son," she chided.

"Yes, we should walk faster. It is going to rain," Brother Hubbard confirmed by looking at the darkening of the clouds. "Might get some damage out here." He pointed to the dark gray sky. "Look at the storm that is brewing. The wind is picking up too. C'mon, Pastor."

Allen let himself be led across the common to their home. As the first drops of rain began to descend on them, they ran the rest of the way. The skies opened and began pouring rain just as they reached the house.

"Whew, we just made it," Sister Hubbard said, helping her children remove their jackets and shoes in the foyer. "Pastor, please have a seat." She pointed off to the right into the living room. "I'm going to check on lunch. It will be ready shortly."

"Well, thank you, Sister Hubbard," said Allen.

"Please call me Jeanette—no need to be so formal."

"Yes, you are family to us," Brother Hubbard said as he removed his trench coat and hung it on the available hook on the wall. "You can call me Lenny." He followed Pastor Allen into the living room. "Would you like some coffee, or would you prefer something cold?"

"I'll have some coffee later, after lunch," Allen said as he rubbed his hands on the arms of the wingback chair he rested in. "Thank you for your hospitality. Sister Hubbard, err, Jeanette, your home is lovely. Everything is so comfortable."

She smiled with her hands folded primly against the front of her skirt. "Just wait until the whirlwind once the kids settle in. I had to threaten them with death to make sure the house stayed clean for your visit."

"Oh, Jeanette, just let the kids be kids. I am nobody special. You said yourself that I'm family," Allen retorted.

"Yes, sir. You will see," Jeanette warned. "Lunch will be ready in about ten minutes. I hope you are hungry."

"Plenty. You know what they say about preachers and Sunday meals, right"? Pastor Allen joked.

"You all sit and keep talking, and I will get everything ready," Jeanette said to the gentlemen then removed herself into the kitchen.

Lenny sat in a wingback chair next to Allen's and slapped his knee. "So, Pastor, you said your old master let you attend Methodist revival services?"

"Yes." Allen leaned in and began to whisper. "They were held at night in the woods. Kind of like secret meetings."

"Your master must have been a believer too then," Lenny said.

"Not at that time. He came to know the Lord later though." Allen's voice trailed as he became entranced in the memory.

He shared about how his life had changed when his master found religion and about how his mother and father had been sold away when his master had come to believe slavery was wrong.

"I told everyone I met about Jesus, yet I had failed to introduce my master to Him." Allen shook his head. "I was so wrapped in my own hatred toward him that I missed the opportunity to love him enough to share Jesus with him. Since I was seven years old, I had been a field hand. I listened to the older slaves and took in their vitriol toward the master. I did not want to see him serve the Lord. I wanted to keep hating him."

"I can see why you might," Lenny confided.

"I remember walking past the slave auctions near the London Coffeehouse. I saw such terrible sights—the public slave sales, families being separated, and the slave shackles protecting masters from slaves' tendency to run. Old Master Chew was an attorney—an important man who sold slaves his entire life. He came to know the Lord and somehow all that changed. He didn't want to own slaves anymore. That's how we ended up going to Stokely Sturgis's plantation where we put crops forward. Indeed, slavery was a bitter pill."

Allen recounted his years of bondage.

"Even as a teenager, I had already seen the horrors of slavery, including the sale of my own mother. Master Sturgis did not keep her long. His farm in Delaware needed people to clear the forests mainly to allow business growth." Allen fought the swell of tears in his eyes and the lump in his throat.

Lenny leaned forward, placing his hand on Allen's knee. "Pastor, what is it? Are you unwell."

Allen waved him off. "Just remembering seeing my mother for the last time. My momma, two of my brothers, and a sister were sold away. As was often the case, we never saw or heard from them again. My papa and the rest of us were heartbroken. We often thought after our master's death we would be sold to the highest bidder—Sturgis was much in debt. Thus, my troubles were increased, and I was often brought to weep between the porch and the altar. In confusion and grief, I searched for answers. It was only the love of God that sustained me."

"I hear you, Pastor. I guess I'll never know that being since I was born free." Lenny wiped a tear from his eye, then shook himself and stood. "Honey, is lunch ready yet?" he called to his wife.

Jeanette emerged from the kitchen carrying a casserole pan. "I was just getting ready to call you all to the dining room. Kids, come and eat," Jeanette yelled upstairs for her children's attention.

The dining room table was well-apportioned with glassware and silverware near the plates. Candles had been lit and stood at the center of the table.

"My goodness, Jeanette. I hope you did not go to any trouble," Allen said as he took his place in the middle of the table in an ornately carved chair.

"Oh, it is not trouble at all. It is only black-eyed peas, some collard greens, and a pork roast—nothing fancy. And I made a pound cake for dessert."

After lunch concluded, the children grew antsy.

"Momma, can Pastor Allen give us a horsey-back ride?" the elder daughter asked sweetly.

"No, I do not think so, Japraunika. Pastor is tired from preaching this morning."

"You don't answer for me. If that baby wants a horseback ride, I will give her one." Allen removed the black suit jacket revealing a white shirt underneath covered by a vest, then got down on all fours and the children climbed aboard. Allen even neighed for them as they stumbled about the room. The six-year-old young boy kicked as if he was wearing spurs.

After about ten minutes, Jeanette said it was time for the children to take their afternoon naps."

"Oh, but mother!" Japraunika whined in protest. "We don't wanna take a nap."

"Naptime, little lady. Take your little brother upstairs."

Once the kids had retired to their bedroom, Jeanette showed Pastor Allen back to the living room for dessert and coffee.

"Oh, thank you, Jeanette." Allen received the saucer in his left hand. He set the plate on the lampstand. He set his dessert plate to the side and then took the coffee cup from Jeanette.

"Pastor was telling me about his memories of passing the slave auction at London Coffeehouse," Lenny said before biting into his pound cake.

"It was very brutal, but we were bound to a man who viewed bondage as vital to business, society, and culture. So much for the brotherly love, huh?" Allen said.

"I really do not wish to talk about this. Perhaps there is a happier conversation to have," Jeanette said.

Allen did not acknowledge Sister Hubbard's concerns. "Master Sturgis ultimately offered the chance for my brother and I to be freed through a process called *delayed manumission*, which basically allowed me to pay $2,000 continental dollars over time to be freed. So, there I was, almost twenty years old, and I was responsible for myself for the first time in my life." Allen held up his fork. "I pledged to become an outspoken advocate against slavery. I would use my platform as a voice for freedom."

Allen set down his now empty plate and reached for his coffee cup. "I was free, but what to do with it? This was the question that I had wrestled with. I was not sure until I read Psalm 68."

He set down his cup and turned to his black Bible. He began to read aloud.

"Let God arise, let his enemies be scattered: let them also that hate him flee before him. As smoke is driven away, so drive them away: as wax melteth before the fire, so let the wicked perish at the presence of God. But let the righteous be glad; let them rejoice before God: yea, let them exceedingly rejoice. Sing unto God, sing praises to his name: extol him that rideth upon the heavens by his name Jah, and rejoice before him. A father of the fatherless, and a judge of the widows, is God in his holy habitation. God setteth the solitary in families: he bringeth out those which are bound with chains: but the rebellious dwell in a dry land. O God, when thou wentest forth before thy people, when thou didst march through the wilderness; Selah: The earth shook, the heavens also dropped at the presence of God: even Sinai itself was moved at the presence of God, the God of Israel. Thou, O God, didst send a plentiful rain, whereby thou didst confirm thine inheritance, when it was weary. Thy congregation hath dwelt therein: thou, O God, hast prepared of thy goodness for the poor. The Lord gave the word: great was the company of those that published it. Kings of armies did flee apace: and she that tarried at home divided the spoil. Though ye have lien among the pots yet shall ye be as the wings of a dove covered with silver, and her feathers with yellow gold. When the Almighty scattered kings in it, it was white as snow in Salmon. The hill of God is as the hill of Bashan, a high hill as the hill of Bashan. Why leap ye, ye high hills? This is the hill which God desireth to dwell in; yea, the Lord will dwell in it for ever. The chariots of God are twenty thousand, even thousands of angels: the Lord is among them, as in Sinai, in the holy place. Thou hast ascended on high, thou hast led captivity captive: thou hast received gifts for men; yea, for the rebellious also, that the Lord God might dwell among them. Blessed be the Lord, who daily loadeth us with benefits, even the God of our salvation. Selah. He that is our God is the God of salvation; and unto God the Lord belong the issues from death. But God shall wound the head of his enemies, and the hairy scalp of such a one as goeth on still in his trespasses.

The Lord said, I will bring again from Bashan, I will bring my people again from the depths of the sea: That thy foot may be dipped in the blood of thine enemies, and the tongue of thy dogs in the same. They have seen thy goings, O God; even the goings of my God, my King, in the sanctuary. The singers went before, the players on instruments followed; among them were the damsels playing with timbrels. Bless ye God in the congregations, even the Lord, from the fountain of Israel. There is little Benjamin with their ruler, the princes of Judah and their council, the princes of Zebulun, and the princes of Naphtali. Thy God hath commanded thy strength: strengthen, O God, that which thou hast wrought for us. Because of thy temple at Jerusalem shall kings bring presents unto thee. Rebuke the company of spearmen, the multitude of the bulls, with the calves of the people, till everyone submit himself with pieces of silver: scatter thou the people that delight in war. Princes shall come out of Egypt; Ethiopia shall soon stretch out her hands unto God. Sing unto God, ye kingdoms of the earth; O sing praises unto the Lord; Selah: To him that rideth upon the heavens of heavens, which were of old; lo, he doth send out his voice, and that a mighty voice. Ascribe ye strength unto God: his excellency is over Israel, and his strength is in the clouds. O God, thou art terrible out of thy holy places: the God of Israel is he that giveth strength and power unto his people. Blessed be God."

Allen shut his book and turned to his hosts.

"Now let me explain why this scripture spoke to me. I do believe the Lord's anger burns against slaveowners. I have heard someone say, 'there is a curse upon the plantation class.' I can honestly say God is on the side of the oppressed. So many scriptures explain his disdain."

"I believe that to be true, Pastor"," Lenny echoed his agreement.

"But in this scripture here, David celebrated God's rule over and care of his people. It foreshadows Christ's destruction of evil and the evil one at the end of the world, and the triumph of all believers in Christ as they rejoice in God's presence."

"You see, David celebrates God as the king who rode majestically before the Israelites as they made their way from slavery in Egypt through the wilderness into the Promised Land in Canaan and who later took his place in the sanctuary on Mount Zion."

"But Pastor, you mentioned other scriptures where the Lord condemned slavery. What are some of those? I don't see that specific thing in Psalm 68."

Lenny was brave to admit his confusion, and Allen smiled at his friend.

"Well, let's look at Isaiah 58 then. The Lord is giving instructions regarding the true purpose for fasting. This chapter begins in verse one with the instruction to 'Cry aloud and spare not.' He is telling me—at least that's how I take it—to not mince words. He indicates why we fast in verse six."

Allen opened his Bible again and began to read.

"Is not this the fast that I have chosen? To loosen the bands of wickedness, to undo the heavy burdens, and to let the oppressed go free, and that ye break every yoke? Is it not to deal thy bread to the hungry, and that thou bring the poor that are cast out to thy house? When thou seest the naked, that thou cover him; and that thou hide not thyself from thine own flesh? Then shall thy light break forth as the morning, and thine health shall spring forth speedily: and thy righteousness shall go before thee; the glory of the Lord shall be thy reward. Then shalt thou call, and the Lord shall answer; thou shalt cry, and he shall say, Here I am. If thou take away from the midst of thee the yoke, the putting forth of the finger, and speaking vanity; And if thou draw out thy soul to the hungry and satisfy the afflicted soul; then shall thy light rise in obscurity, and thy darkness be as the noon day. And the Lord shall guide thee continually, and satisfy thy soul in drought, and make fat thy bones: and thou shalt be like a watered garden, and like a spring of water, whose waters fail not."

"I understand why we fast. 'To break the yoke of oppression' and all. It is very clear, but these are Old Testament scriptures.

Does he condemn slavery in the New Testament?" Lenny probed for more answers.

"Yes, indeed there are some in the New Testament. It can't get any plainer than the Apostle Paul's guidance in Colossians three verse eleven where Paul insists 'there is neither Greek nor Jew, circumcision nor uncircumcision, Barbarian, Scythian, bond nor free: but Christ is all, and in all.'"

"I just can't believe that God was pleased with the slave trade where it involves only colored people," Jeanette chimed in.

"The Bible condemns race-based slavery in that it teaches that all men are created by God and made in His image. And this is where I cry aloud and spare not," Allen affirmed.

Just then, the top step creaked and Japraunika asked, "Mommy, is it alright if we wake up now?"

"Oh, my goodness, look at the time. It is four o'clock already. Yes, baby, you can get up now. Come on downstairs," Jeanette said.

The two children sleepily came down the stairs. Their eyes lit up when they realized Pastor Allen was still in the house.

"Papa's still here!"

Allen enjoyed it when kids called him Papa. The children ran and leaped at the seated Allen who drew them into him in a warm embrace, rubbing the heads of the children.

"Yes, I'm here, but I really need to get moving. Your parents and I have been in deep conversation. I have kept them long enough, and it looks like the rain has stopped. I can walk home without getting soaked. Thank you, Jeanette, for your kindness and hospitality. That cake was delicious."

"Pastor, do you really have to go? We have a guest bedroom. You could spend the night," Lenny offered.

"No, I do need to be on my way." Allen accepted his suit jacket from Brother Hubbard and put his topcoat on in the foyer.

"Good night, Hubbard family. Blessings on this house." Allen pronounced his blessing as he departed. He felt he had 'done his job' by sharing the mission to deliver souls from enslavement.

Chapter 2

A New Identity

Standing on the platform at St. George's, Reverend Allen continued explaining his life after he had been freed by Master Sturgis. "I had used all the money I had saved to pay for my freedom. I was penniless," he admitted. "Papa, Momma, and my siblings were all gone, so I packed my belongings, and I made my way south toward Maryland. I carried salt on a wagon with horses. Slavery taught me many trades I could ply when I was alone on the road. There, indeed, were some hungry days, but the good Lord saw fit to draw me out of the slavery way. I was determined to live for Him. I also heard there were men who paid their way by preaching at different church meetings, so I figured I could do that too."

"Yessuh!" a male congregant added his voice.

"While I was out there preaching. I met Reverend Francis Asbury, another Methodist minister. He asked me to join him in the mission to save America's souls. I gladly accepted the position as his special assistant. Asbury preached in myriad of places—courthouses, public houses, tobacco houses, fields, public squares, wherever a crowd assembled to hear him. I had ridden some six thousand miles with him from New York to Maryland and Phil-adelphia. He praised my astonishing preaching abilities."

Allen waited until the voices amening calmed down.

"Asbury told me one evening, 'I would be remiss if I didn't take a moment, as a white minister, to reflect on what knowing you has done for me personally. The book of Nehemiah begins with Nehemiah confessing to God the sins of his forefathers, and I should be able to do the same both for myself and the people I represent.' He'd lowered his head before continuing.

"'I am deeply saddened by the way the Church has institutionalized racism and used God to deepen the divide between themselves and brothers and sisters, like you, Richard Allen. We have sinned against you in word and deed through what we've done and left undone. We've not loved with our whole hearts, and we justly deserve your anger. I am sorry, and I hope for your forgiveness so we can move toward reconciliation that Jesus has won for us with the cross.'"

Allen stopped his story and smiled. "He embraced me that day, and I fully embraced him. Forgiveness was not mine alone to give, but I embraced him as my brother in Christ."

There was a brief round of applause in the auditorium.

"Through my association with Asbury, I had opportunity to meet Thomas Garrett, a famous abolitionist. Garrett gave me this here Bible." Allen held up the small black book for the audience to see. "Reverend Asbury wanted me to go to North Carolina with him. I told him no because the slave counties scared the mess out of me. I came back to Delaware instead."

"Amen. Right where you belong," a parishioner added.

"By that time, old Master Sturgis had been having revival meetings at his house. In the summer of 1779, several ministers had come to speak there, including Asbury. As it should, the word of God absolutely melted Sturgis's heart. After that, he could not be satisfied to hold slaves. In fact, he put it into writing."

Richard unfolded a piece of paper and read from it.

"'I do hereby for myself, my heirs, executors, administrators or assigns manumit, exonerate, release and forever discharge and set at full liberty said Negro man named Richard quitting all claim that I were they in my right or might have to him by virtue of any law, custom, or usage whatsoever.'"

Allen folded the paper back up and slid it back into his Bible. The congregation applauded the letter amid shouts of "Praise the Lord" and celebratory "Yes" or "Thank You, Jesus." Allen waited until those gathered had grown silent before continuing.

"I would never be known as Negro Richard like I had been in my past. With the stroke of Sturgis's pen and God's help, that had been wiped away. On that day, I adopted the name Richard Allen. I had been reborn. Praise the Lord."

The audience erupted in applause shouting, "Praise the Lord!"

Once again, Allen waited for them to settle.

"Sturgis made sure to give me a pass, allowing for unfettered travel near and far. I continued preaching and working. I carried salt to the revolutionary forces and sure to have services along the way. I never forgot to serve my Lord. I used off-times to pray, sitting, standing, or lying."

"For the next year or so, I lived with several of my white preacher colleagues in New Jersey. I walked until my feet became so sore I blistered. I could scarcely bear them to the ground. I became convinced that blacks and whites could pray together, eat together, and live together as equals in the new republic. So here we are in 1785." Allen paused for effect. "I just stopped by to tell you this is reconciliation. This is how we build our country. Together."

The audience shouted and stomped their feet and began to cheer "Together. Together."

After a few moments of this boisterous shouting, Allen held up his hand for silence.

"Many of you in this room do not share my experience having been a slave for you are free born. That matters not when you understand 2 Corinthians 5:19 where Paul explains that God was in Christ and reconciled the world unto himself, not imputing their trespasses unto them; and having committed unto us the word of reconciliation."

"You must be able to see the brute and the beggar as you see God because he is made in the image of God. The man who may have owned some of you requires you to love him and for you to see God in him. This is the word of reconciliation that God wants us to share with the world. The man who called you nigger is not your enemy, he just needs a heart change. You need to see things from beyond a black-white polemic and beyond a white is wrong, black is right perspective. We did not arrive on the same boat, but we are all in this together. Can I get an amen?"

"Amen" echoed around the church. "Amen, Brother."

Chapter 3

WILL YOU JOIN US?

"Absolutely masterful sermon, Pastor," the older white man said while approaching Pastor Allen later that day. "Well done. I teared up. I was so inspired. I knew you were the one."

"Thank you, sir." Allen looked quizzically at the white man complimenting him. "I'm sorry, I'm not sure I know your name, sir."

"Oh, I am sorry. I failed to introduce myself. I am Reverend Louis Livingston. I pastor a church here in the Philadelphia proper area. I was in the audience listening to your message about reconciliation, and I said 'Lord, this must be the one.'"

Allen wrinkled his brow. "The one? The one for what?"

"To help me. I have been praying and asking the Lord to show me the man to help me, and he brought me to you."

"Let's go into the church office to talk." Allen led the way into the rear of the barn where the congregation had been meeting—remnants of his time as an itinerant evangelist. Allen moved the hay bales sitting in the way then invited the gentleman to sit on the hay with him.

Once they were seated facing each other, Allen asked, "Ah, Pastor Livingston, what may I help you with?"

Livingston looked over his shoulder as if he were worried

someone may overhear. Then he leaned in closer. "How ... how do you win a colored man to the Lord?"

Allen laughed. "The same way you win a white man. There's really no difference."

Livingston chuckled and sat back on the hay bale. "Maybe I said it the wrong way. Let me tell you what is going on. In my congregation, we have about fifty colored people who have been attending our services, and the white people are starting to feel uneasy. I am thinking about doing a separate service for them, but I felt like they need someone of like kind to provide spiritual care. That's where you come in."

Allen frowned. "I'll tell you, honestly, sir. Your question borders on the offensive."

Livingston hemmed and hawed. "I never meant to offend, Pastor. I just think they need something I cannot give them."

Allen retorted, "And I somehow do? What gives you that idea? My brown skin? I do not even know your people. Just because we are 'like kind'—as you have said—does not guarantee I am the right person to lead them."

Pastor Livingston held up a hand. "The idea that 'like kind' provides is you are likely more familiar with their unique needs and how to support them. You were once a slave. I cannot empathize. I would likely represent the enslaver more than a spiritual leader. Many of our colored are former slaves. We do have some free folks—born free." He paused and looked Allen right in the eye. "How do I get them to trust me?"

Emboldened, Allen said, "Separating is not the way to do that. You asked me how to win a colored man. That question proves to me you haven't done the first things."

"What do you mean by 'first things'?" Livingston wrung his hat in his hands as he waited for the reply.

"I'll tell you. Let me ask you this, how often do you go to their houses for a meal? How much time do you spend with your colored flock outside of official church times? That's where trust is built. I bet you haven't even talked to them. Communication is central to growth. White people who have little to no interaction with black folks act like colored folk are aliens and speak a different language to the extent that they think communication between races somehow must be different. Your colored congregation is no different, wants nothing different other than to feel the love of Jesus spread to them. No more, no less."

Livingston sighed. "That is why I think you are the right person. We need truth tellers. Someone who is not shy to tell the truth. Someone who will not be afraid to tell the white people—including me—the truth. It's the only way." The older man raised his eyebrows. "Will you join me?"

Allen shook his head. "I don't feel like God has called me back to Philadelphia or to your congregation." He could see Livingston's defeat as he slumped against the barn wall. "However, I will pray on it."

Livingston sat up straight once more, hope in his eyes. "I understand. It is a tall order. You are right to pray on it. It's not permanent, though. Perhaps only for a few months."

"I will tell you what I will do," Allen suggested. "How about I visit once, and we go from there? I'll preach, and we'll see how the congregation responds to my presence. All right?"

"They will love you, undoubtedly." Livingston smiled and vigorously shook Allen's hand.

A little over a month later, Allen stood to address the forty or so black congregants and the other white folks in Livingston's Methodist church. He wore a black waistcoat and white shirt tied with a cravat. On this day, his average, five-feet-four-inch frame seemed giant standing in the pulpit. His demeanor quiet and stoic, his smile amiable. He was the picture of grace.

Pastor Livingston had introduced him already and told the congregation to treat the visiting preacher well, so they could possibly convince him to stay longer.

Allen grinned at those gathered, then began. "Good morning, saints, and praise the Lord." Allen's voice boomed with gravitas despite his only twenty-six years. "My objective today is to show that the purposes of the enemy and the Messiah are in direct conflagration for your soul! The Messiah wants victorious life eternal for you. The devil wants to share eternal life with you also—for your utter destruction. Everything you are as a created, submitted servant of God, is an affront to Lucifer's rebellion against God. Anyone that has the freedom of choice to serve God is a threat to the devil."

A few quiet "amens" could be heard throughout the crowd—nothing like the boisterous congregation Allen was used to. These folks were still yet unsure of this guest preacher.

He turned to the Bible in his right hand. "My first text today is Zechariah 9:9. Take a moment to look it up. When you get to the passage, say amen. If you need more time, say wait a minute."

A few people chuckled, and he smiled to himself. *Laughter is the way to the heart.* When most had said amen and none had asked him to wait, he dug into the text.

"Rejoice greatly, O daughter of Zion; shout, O daughter of Jerusalem: behold thy King cometh unto thee: he is just, and having salvation, lowly, and riding upon an ass, and upon a colt the foal of an ass.

"A donkey was a burden-bearer, you see. And Jesus was about to bear our burdens on the cross of Calvary. The Old Testament prophecy of Zechariah was fulfilled now of Jesus's triumphant entry into Jerusalem. This is not just a fulfillment of Old Testament prophecy, but an indication of what Jesus wants to do in your life."

"Yes," an older man in the front pew cosigned.

Allen nodded and smiled at the man before continuing. "Turn now to Matthew 21:8–11. Listen while I read these words. 'And a very great multitude spread their garments in the way; others cut down branches from the trees, and strawed them in the way. And the multitudes that went before, and that followed, cried, saying,

Hosanna to the Son of David: Blessed is he that cometh in the name of the Lord; Hosanna in the highest. And when he was come into Jerusalem, all the city was moved, saying, 'Who is this?' And the multitude said, 'This is Jesus the prophet of Nazareth of Galilee.'"

"Yes, Lord!" a solitary voice rang out.

"His employment of this prophesy is intentional," Allen continued. "We think that many of the prophetic fulfillments—there are over three hundred and fifty Old Testament prophecies of the Messiah—were happenstance. They were not! They were intentionally fulfilled. Jesus knew the Scripture in Zechariah when he stood on the mount of Olives at Bethpage and told his disciples to go get the donkey, that this would be a fulfillment of Zechariah's prophecy. God has always been intentional. Jesus had a purpose in every miracle, every parable, every doctrinal teaching. Much of it was to point to Him being Messiah. The healing of the leper, the opening of the blind eyes, the lame man walking. Every miracle was intentional!"

"Yes!"

"Amen, brother!"

To Allen, the cheers made him feel the audience was beginning to trust him. He smiled. The more he smiled, and the more feedback he received, the more confident he grew. He stood tall behind the pulpit now.

"Let me give you a little background. You see, six days before the Passover, Jesus arrived in Bethany, the home of Lazarus— the man he had raised from the dead. A dinner was prepared in Jesus's honor. Martha served, and Lazarus sat at the table with him. Then Mary took a twelve-ounce jar of expensive perfume, and she anointed Jesus's feet with it and wiped his feet with her hair. And the house was filled with fragrance. But that old slewfoot, Judas Iscariot, one of his chosen disciples—the one who would betray him—said that perfume was worth a small fortune. It should have been sold and the money given to the poor. He didn't care one bit for the poor. He was a thief who oversaw the disciples' funds, and he often took some for his own use."

Allen paused while the congregants issued their views of Judas aloud.

He continued, "Jesus replied, 'Let her be. She is preparing me for my burial. You will always have the poor among you, but I will not be here with you much longer.' The next day, the news that Jesus was on the way to Jerusalem swept through the city. A huge crowd of Passover visitors took palm branches and went down the road to meet him. They shouted 'Praise God! Bless the one who comes in the name of the Lord! Hail to the King of Israel!'"

"Hosanna in the highest!"

"Yes, that's right," Reverend Allen said to his new amen corner. Their interactions delighted him. "All our discussion and theology concerning Jesus, all our reasons for being a Christian, all our efforts to 'do church,' are without purpose and merit unless we understand that everything we do relates to Jesus triumphantly and victoriously entering the life of the individual! And that he does intentionally in our lives."

"C'mon, preacher! Say that!" a man seated on the deacon's pew shouted enthusiastically.

"Let me bring this to a conclusion. John 10:10 says 'The thief cometh not, but for to steal, and to kill, and to destroy I am come that they might have life, and that they might have it more abundantly.' Every purpose of the enemy of our soul is to destroy us. Even the things that seem good which the devil brings to tempt you are meant to destroy you and your life. The Messiah came to open the blind eyes, to bring out the prisoners from the prison, and to bring them that sit in darkness out of the prison house. Some of you sitting here are fresh off the plantation, you bear the scars of America's original sin on your back. I stopped by to tell you that I'm the preacher to help you open your eyes and to bring you out of this prison you're in. I'm the preacher to absolve America of that sin. There's only one way. Let me show you the love of God."

The mixed-race congregation was astonished by Allen's words. Some of them sat with mouths agape while Allen made a final, special appeal.

"Take your neighbor by the hand and join me here at the altar. Let's pray together. It's the only solution to heal the hearts." When Allen noticed the congregants looking skeptical of his command, he waved his hand, gesturing them forward. "Come and let all this racial foolishness be washed away."

Pastor Livingston smiled warmly, stood, and grabbed a colored man's hand, and together they walked toward the altar. Soon they were joined by several other parishioners. Pastor Allen prayed over those that had been bold enough to gather at the altar but noticed some—both white and black—had left the church building.

Chapter 4

A New Commission

Allen soon settled back in his hometown of Philadelphia and made plans to build a better society. This burgeoning society needs a leader. He set his intentions on institutionalizing the society he dreamed of with churches, reform groups, and educational societies.

This is the way to secure equality for blacks, but first I must build their souls. If I want to build a better world, I'm going to start converting blacks to God first.

He fully intended to find sanction for his version of Afro-Christianity. Today, he stood in front of the elder Methodist pastor at Livingston's church, talking about his vision for their community.

"Most free blacks conduct their lives reputably," the older white minister said. "Some of them are very worthy citizens. That's why we want to create an abolitionist society—to protect them and the cause of antislavery. I believe we can help those running from the rural areas here in Pennsylvania, Maryland, New Jersey, and Virginia. It is important that black people have good role models to aspire to and emulate, like you. You have worked as a dry goods dealer, a chimney sweep, and a minister."

"It is dirty work, but somebody's got to do it," Allen admitted.

"I have heard from another abolitionist you are a hard worker.

But Young Tilghman Fitzgerald, the boy you work with, has made a complaint about you, comparing you almost as a slave master."

"I am insulted by that comparison," Allen said. "Just because I work hard and expect others to be at their best does not justify calling me that. I sincerely live my life to not be associated with the slave trade. For surely, I have seen the afflictions of my people, and I have heard their cries by reason of their taskmasters. I am come to deliver."

"You have already run off the Tilghman boy."

"He just didn't want to work. Am I so wrong to expect work be done?" Allen defended. His gaze was distracted by the sight of an old friend walking down the street. "Oh, look, there's my friend, Absalom. He and I have talked about starting a nail factory together. Isn't that right, Absalom?"

His older friend Absalom Jones walked up to the pair. "Sure is. We may be able to find some indentures to apprentice with us."

"Yes, we can teach them to be humble and pious, and how to walk like free men," Allen agreed. "We will be able to teach them how to handle discrimination in the workplace, inadequate public schooling, and segregated church pews. For it is religion," Allen argued, "that will provide the moral discipline to survive white prejudice. Indeed, piety and industrious go hand in hand. We must admonish them to value hard work and diligence. For the enemies of freedom use the perception of idle laziness as cause to why we ought not be free."

The older white minister nodded, then said, "Perhaps you can do the same thing at St. George's that you did in Baltimore? Offer a 5:00 a.m. service on Sundays for coloreds," the elder Methodist minister proffered. "I know it's early, but I just know the people will be charged by your preaching."

On the following Sunday morning, Reverend Allen addressed the small number of congregants at the 5:00 a.m. service.

"The title of my sermon this morning is 'Every Scar a Story.'" Allen paused, then began to pace behind the pulpit. "I had a weird dream, and it was about you all. I dreamed about starting a new congregation—an all-black church."

The few people that were gathered praised and cheered.

Allen moved back behind the pulpit and opened his Bible. "For my text this morning, we are going to read the Gospel of John chapter twenty and begin at verse nineteen. We'll read down to twenty-one. When you have it, say amen." He waited for the parishioners to flip pages and for the amens to slow before reading

"'Then the same day at evening, being the first day of the week, when the doors were shut where the disciples were assembled for fear of the Jews, came Jesus and stood in the midst, and saith unto them, 'Peace be unto you.' And when he had so said, he shewed unto them his hands and his side. Then were the disciples glad when they saw the Lord. Then said Jesus to them again, 'Peace be unto you: as my Father hath sent me, even so send I you.'"

Allen looked up from his Bible to the eager faces of his congregation.

"On my back are scars from whippings I received as a slave. You probably have scars of your own."

"Amen. Sure do," a gentleman in the congregation answered.

"Today, I want to talk about the power of scars. Scars are a natural part of the body's healing process. A scar results from a wound repairing itself—the skin and other tissues. Most wounds, except for very minor ones, result in some degree of scarring. Scars can result from accidents, diseases, skin conditions, and, yes, even whippings."

He had to pause a moment to shake off the many beatings he'd received at Sturgis's plantation. Then he continued.

"We don't like them, these scars. We don't want them. We are ashamed of them. We want to avoid them at all costs. But wounds happen. When wounds heal, scars form. This is a fact of life. We scar because we are wounded. We scar, and our bodies are never quite the same after we are wounded. Our wounds can embitter us and destroy us, or they can heal and strengthen us.

"Scars are nothing more than the new growth of skin at the place where we have suffered some sort of injury. And yet, scars are more than that. Sometimes when I visit former slaves, they insist on showing me their scars. One reason I believe we feel compelled to show our scars to each other is to show that an experience happened, that it was real. Scars tell a story that something really happened."

"It's true, brother," yelled a man as he held up his right hand to show the scar there.

"In John's gospel, the resurrected Jesus reveals himself before his disciples, and to prove he is the resurrected Lord, He shows the disciples his hands and his side—like my brother in Christ back there has just done for us. Jesus had been pierced by nails through his hands and feet. And a soldier had pierced Jesus's side with a spear. The scars told his story. This person standing before the disciples had been crucified in the most inhumane way, and yet now … here he stands. He had died, and yet he lived. The scars tell a story that really happened. In our lives we have all sorts of scars—physical, mental, emotional, and maybe even spiritual scars. Our scars may run very deep. There may be scars we don't want anyone to see or know about. And we wonder if our wounds will ever really heal."

"Yes. True, true," someone cosigned.

"Oftentimes, our bodies heal better and stronger than they were before they were wounded. Such is the case with a bone. This is certainly true with our spiritual and emotional scars. Just as any piece of leather has its own unique character and beauty because of the scars on it, so our wounds and the resulting spiritual and emotional scars in our lives can add to the character and beauty of our lives. As we heal from emotional and spiritual wounds, we are made into stronger, deeper people. Our character is strengthened, and our spirits deepened."

Allen paused to let the thought sink in. He knew he needed some kind of tangible comparison.

"If you've ever had a bad cut and had a scar form as it healed, did you ever notice how the scar tissue is much tougher than the skin around it? I've got a lot of physical scars to prove this fact, and I bet you do too. When we're damaged emotionally or spiritually, the scars of Christ can heal our damaged spirit and make us stronger. Tougher, like that skin."

"Amen. Thank you, Jesus!" a bonneted woman called out, her right hand lifted to heaven.

"Do you remember the story of Thomas in John chapter twenty?" Allen asked. "How he wouldn't believe Jesus had risen until he saw the scars in his hand? Notice something important at this point—Jesus didn't hesitate to show Thomas the scars. He held his hand out and even let Thomas touch them. Put his fingers in them.

"We possibly all have physical scars. Scars that mark a fateful fall down a steep slope, scars that mark a fall on our knees, scars that indicate childbirth, perhaps even scars of a failed attempt to take our own life in one way or the other. When we look at a scar, the first thing most of us think of is how ugly it is. How it breaks up the smoothness of our skin or disrupts an even line. Where the ugliness may be true, the scar can be a way to view a life experience—good or bad. Viewing a particular scar, we remember how painful it was when it was inflicted. But remember how that pain has subsided and is now gone with nothing more than a vague memory of the initial pain. More than anything, we hopefully remember not to go there again, not to push the envelope so to speak or simply to be more careful … next time."

Allen sensed by their constant amens that the audience clearly had received his words.

He continued, "Now, think about the spiritual scars in our lives. Have we had times in our lives that we would rather erase from memory? Remember a time when you were flat on your back and could do nothing but look up? No one seemed to care or understand what you were going through. You got up. You did recover, and you probably experienced a defining moment that would bring you to the next stage in your life as a result." Allen looked out over the sea of nodding heads, knowing he'd struck a chord. "When we realize no one was there for us, we realized He was there all the time." Here he pointed his finger toward the ceiling. "He was all we had, and He was all we needed. You know what your scars mean?" He pointed now at the congregation. "They mean you are healed. What once hurt you no longer hurts."

Richard could see several people tearing up now. His message was sinking in. The Father had led him well today.

"Looking on all my scars, I can choose to remember when it happened—it really did—or I can remember this. I may have scars, but I am healed."

A silence fell over the crowd as Allen let his last words sink in.

Then he clapped his hands and said, "Join me at the altar. Let's all pray for healing from our scars. Let's accept the healing that comes from a forgiving spirit."

Chapter 5

He Changed Me
1786–7

Great message, today, Pastor," Absalom raved after one of the morning services.

"Which part did you like the best, brother?"

"The part where you connected people's slavery stories to their memories. You said that Jesus cleanses us from all wickedness, and that he will forgive us if we forgive. He doesn't just cleanse but forgives us and this includes all the wounds we have taken on ourselves." A small group of congregants had cornered Allen after service. "He's doing something in us through his blood even beyond what Calvary's main purpose was—to save our souls. I'll be honest, I'm trying to forgive my old master, but I cannot forget, and that makes me angry every time I think of it."

"That just means you still have some forgiving to do, brother." Allen slapped him on the back. "You must follow Paul's plan where he said we must die daily. God also said we must confess our sin to him, and he will be faithful and just to forgive us and cleanse us of all unrighteousness. We need to get to the very core of our souls and that is what forgiveness does. In the model prayer, Jesus said we are to 'forgive us trespasses as we forgive those who have trespassed against us.' You must let pain of the past go to move to what God wants for you."

Allen and Absalom walked a little farther without comment. When they had reached their destination, Allen turned to his friend and said, "But I'll be honest, brother, I am not sure how long we can sustain with only a few faithful attendees for members. We're giving them the right, good word, but more people need to hear it."

"Right," Absalom agreed. "We'll need to double down, nay, triple down, on our efforts. We need to go out into the 'highways and hedges' to compel them to come. We've got to think of something else." Absalom slid has hand over his hair, slicking it back.

The following Sunday, Allen looked down at the congregation from his vaulted position. There were eight men in the audience. "Today, we'll be talking about God changing Abram's name. I want to remind you of the scripture in 2 Corinthians 5:17. It simply declares 'if any man be in Christ, he is a new creature. Old things are passed away and behold all things are become new.'" He paused while the men gathered flipped pages so they could verify the Bible verse.

"See, his name had been Abram. But in Genesis 17:5, the Lord changed it. 'Neither shall thy name any more be called Abram, but thy name shall be Abraham; for a father of many nations have I made thee.' Now, we don't know why God changed his name to Abraham. He changed Simon Peter to just Peter in the Book of Matthew too. But the new name expresses a new nature. It is a memorial of victory. This change of name is indicative of the spirit of a life's work. I know that's why I am no longer called Negro Richard. The spirit has work for me to do, but it is the Lord's work now and not my master's. Let's look at Ephesians 4:17–24."

Allen waited until the men flipped pages again, then began to read.

"'This I say therefore, and testify in the Lord, that ye henceforth walk not as other Gentiles walk, in the vanity of their mind, Having the understanding darkened, being alienated from the life of God through the ignorance that is in them, because of the blindness of their heart: Who being past feeling have given themselves over unto lasciviousness, to work all uncleanness with greediness. But ye have not so learned Christ; If so be that ye have heard him, and have been taught by him, as the truth is in Jesus. That ye put off concerning the former conversation the old man, which is corrupt according to the deceitful lusts; And be renewed in the spirit of your mind; And that ye put on the new man, which after God is created in righteousness and true holiness.'

"Remember what God said in Ezekiel 36:26? The word says, 'A new heart also will I give you, and a new spirit will I put within you: and I will take away the stony heart out of your flesh, and I will give you an heart of flesh.' That's why Brother Absalom and I started the Free African Society. We didn't want to be former slaves but known as free."

The men gathered nodded in agreement. He had them. Now, if he could just get others to join too.

In a little over a month's time at St. George's, they had managed to add to the regular attendees about forty colored members. The senior pastor then decided he wanted to try mixing the congregation again. Allen agreed to give it a try, but soon the white people grew uncomfortable with the number of "uppity" blacks—a word he'd heard muttered—attending. Allen and St. George's pastor disagreed about the level of discomfort. He wanted to keep trying, but Allen feared retribution if they continued.

Chapter 6

BLACK EXODUS
1787

Good morning, Brother Allen. A fine Sunday morning, isn't it?" Sister Myrtle greeted beneath her beautifully ornate church hat.

"My, my, that is one fancy hat," Allen exclaimed.

"Do you like it? I made it myself." Myrtle beamed with pride as she lightly touched the wide brim of the straw hat adorned with a festive blue ribbon.

"She's trying to curry favor with God by getting noticed with that hat on," Sister Jeter joked to another woman.

"That's not neighborly or Christian-like, Sister," Allen chided, offering Sister Jeter a wink then turned to Sister Myrtle. "The sun is almost outshined by that glorious hat you're wearing, Sister Myrtle. Shall we go inside to pray?"

"Yes. Let's do." Sister Myrtle nodded as she ushered her black women friends into St. George's.

"Lordamercy! Everybody is already here," Myrtle said as she ducked her large hat with its wide brim underneath the door jamb.

There were blacks aplenty this morning. Sister Jackson was there with her tribe of children—all eight of them—the youngest ones crawling all over the pew. Other families Allen had met took up a lot of the seats, and he noticed some white ushers speaking to some of the blacks. Perhaps they were finally coming around. The ushers took time to ask the seated blacks to move to the balcony.

But as they entered the sanctuary, a white usher directed his group to stand along the wall instead of going to their regular seats.

"Oh, we can't be seated? Y'all starting this nonsense in the house of the Lord?" Sister Myrtle said with a scowl.

"I'm tired of this," said a flustered Sister Jeter. "We aren't taking up that much room."

Allen held up a hand and waited to see what the usher would do. Certainly, we're not going to stand here. There are perfectly good seats still available.

Before long, the usher directed them to seats in the balcony. Allen noticed the other white ushers were doing the same with those already seated.

Sister Jackson did not appreciate having to pack up her children from the pews they already occupied. Allen watched as she scolded this one and that, then sent a scowl toward the usher who was waiting impatiently by.

"This is just ridiculous. I want to be closer to God, but I am not sure this is the way to do it. What do you say, Brother Allen?" sixteen-year-old Bernard Jackson questioned as they made their way to the balcony seats.

"Let's just kneel and pray. No need to make a spectacle," Brother Allen told him. "We are going to need the Lord's help today. Perhaps the Lord will intervene? Or at least give us instructions on what to do."

Allen knelt to pray with his head bowed deeply, singing a hymn to himself. As he pleaded with the Lord, he felt distracted by the sounds of the ushers making demands, insisting the blacks below in the pews move. He opened his eyes and saw an usher with his hands on Absalom's shoulders. The usher tugged at his friend's jacket as he refused the usher's demands.

"You must not kneel here—you need to get up," Allen heard the usher say.

Allen watched the white people around Absalom as they

witnessed this altercation. He wanted just one person to stop being so pious and come to his friend's aid, but no one spoke up. The white people just stared. Someone started singing loudly in an attempt to drown out the conflict.

Defiant, Jones pulled against the usher's demand.

"By whose authority are you acting today, sir? Wait until prayer is over and then I will move," Jones said.

The usher pulled away a moment, clearly agitated. His red face belied the serious black uniform he wore. Allen wondered why his face was so severe but breathed a sigh of relief as the white man walked away. Satisfied they would be left alone, Allen again closed his eyes. Incredulous as to what had just happened, he tried to center himself in prayer.

Suddenly the commotion grew louder, and Allen once again opened his eyes. The white usher had asserted his insistence that Absalom move from his position and was now forcibly moving his friend.

The commotion was enough for the other black onlookers to be roused to their feet from their prayers. The crowd quickly grew angry at what they were witnessing.

"Brother Allen, let's go," said Sister Myrtle, wiping at the tears that had welled in her eyes with a handkerchief she had pulled from her purse. "This maltreatment is uncalled for. They obviously don't want us here. Let's just go."

As Allen followed Sister Myrtle and Sister Jeter toward the door, he heard Sister Hubbard's two children asking questions.

"Momma, why are we leaving? Why did that man make us get out? We was just trying to pray. I don't understand."

"Japraunika, Brother Allen will get all this straightened out. Not to worry," Sister Hubbard said as she tugged at her little girl's sleeve on her white cotton dress with pink ribbons. She looked at Brother Allen for reassurance.

"I hate being black!" Larry Jr. cried as they made their way to the door.

"Son, let me talk to you." Brother Hubbard knelt next to his son in the stairwell. "I don't ever want to hear you talk like that again. Your black skin is beautiful. Some people may not be able to see it and may judge you harshly for it, but we were made in the image of God."

Allen chimed in. "Your father is right, Little Larry. When God designed you and me and your momma and daddy, he said we were good. He said that to every person here, no matter their color. We are all handcrafted by God. We've got nothing to be ashamed of or sorry for." He patted Larry on the head and playfully smacked his bottom. "Now, smile." The boy smiled up at Allen, then departed from the church, skipping down the stairs two at a time.

Ordinarily, the ladies attempted to quell the sound of their shoes on the stairs. Today, they practically stomped down the stairs as they left the church balcony as one loud body. They were not concerned with the white ministers who merely stood by and let this spectacle happen. Nor were they overly concerned with the white citizens in attendance.

"I don't care how they feel about it. We are free of them," an angry sister announced as she clomped her way toward the door.

"I mean, how dare they treat us as common slaves. We are free people. I never imagined being so mistreated in a church," Brother William Gray said as he followed the loud ladies.

"It matters not that we are not slaves. No one deserves to be treated like that in the house of the Living God," Allen said. "I have been a slave and stand against this maltreatment. Still the whites need not feel plagued by our presence anymore." Allen helped several older ladies down the stairs and toward the door. "Even if we were slaves, no one deserves such treatment. It is a sin before God," he announced to the fifty others who had gathered outside the church. "The Lord has indeed spoken. It's time for us to start our own church. Next week, we will meet at the blacksmith shop down the road. We will never be treated as equals until we have our own church."

"This is just too much to handle," Sister Myrtle said, keeping a tight grip on her adorned hat.

Outside the church building, Allen reached for the hand of the brother on the right. "Let us join together in prayer." He began to wail out a song but only sang a few bars of a familiar hymn before abruptly stopping.

"The Bible declares that we should 'pray for those who despitefully use us.'" he cried out. "Jesus told us in the book of Matthew to 'love your enemies, bless them that curse you, do good to them that hate you and despitefully use you and persecute you.'"

"Amen. He sure did," Brother Absalom shouted from somewhere in the black crowd.

"The people inside that church are not our enemies, they are our brothers and sisters in Christ," cried Allen, pointing one finger back to the now closed church doors. "They might not know it yet, but we do. We should not repay evil for evil, but our primary job is merely to love them. So, if you see your white brother or sister at the market this week, don't think about this today nor remind them of their lack of attention to our cries for fair treatment. Hold no ill will." Allen closed his eyes and prayed, "Heavenly Father, we certainly did not deserve what happened today, but give us the strength to bear up under it. Help us to forgive and help us to remember we are and whose we are. In Jesus's name, amen."

All the people encircled there cried out, "In Jesus's name. Amen."

"And now, saints, we will take our leave. I'll see you next Sunday at the blacksmith shop on Sixth and Lombard Streets. I will get the place ready this week."

Allen stood still as he watched his congregation walk away with their heads held high. When everyone else had gone over the horizon, Allen waved his hands symbolically wiping the dust from his feet before departing himself.

That week, a flurry of work happened as Allen and a few fellow parishioners scurried about converting the blacksmith shop owned by Allen into a makeshift church. They put in a clapboard floor over the dirt space that soaked in the recent rains into a mud consistency. The crew took the final Saturday to clean away the soot remnants from the smithing. With brooms and rags, they spruced the last vestiges away. You could hardly tell its original service in the space. They even installed wooden benches they had fashioned.

On Sunday morning, the saints filed in. Most people came in family groups wearing their Easter Sunday best. Men wore suit jackets and ties while the women wore their hair covered with bonnets or hats.

Soon, someone started a syncopated rhythm by tapping a cane on the clapboard floor. The drumbeat called everyone into an orgasmic rhythm, and they took turns singing and clapping along. An elder female began singing, "Kum by Yah," and that triggered a happy attitude among those gathered. Soon there was no one who was not clapping or stomping their feet—even the children.

Reverend Allen invited everyone to gather in a circle at the front of the church. "Come, let's remember the times we had seeking the Lord at the old praise houses back in the woods. We don't have to be ashamed. We don't have to fear anyone—this is our worship space, and we can glorify God as we see fit."

A person who just recently entered the building immediately began scraping a washboard to match the drumbeat. Another struck in by beating a pie tin as a tambourine. The flat metallic tone rivaled the stick against the floor.

"Oh, what a glorious feeling!" Allen shouted above the din.

Women danced while lifting the hems of their dresses and shouting "Woohoo!" Others praised by yelling "Hallelujah!" They stirred up the praise the more they danced, and one song blended into the next—a song never really concluding before the next one began.

Allen shouted above the merriment, "Sing, children! Ain't nothing wrong with being free! Worship the Lord in the beauty of holiness. Be free!"

The very active praising increased the temperature until sweat rolled down the foreheads of the shouters. Men mopped sweat from their necks and brows, while women fanned themselves with their skirts.

Allen was reminded of the heat in the old blacksmith shop, but this was a different kind of heat. "Oh, sing unto the Lord a new song. Sing unto the Lord all the earth. Sing unto the Lord and bless his name. Show forth his salvation and bless his name and show forth his salvation from day to day. Sing and open the door to heaven!"

When the praising showed signs of slowing down, Allen carried his Bible to the podium and motioned for the saints to take their seats. When they had and were looking up at him expectantly, he began.

"The Apostle Paul wrote to the Galatian church: 'Then fourteen years after I went up again to Jerusalem with Barnabas and took Titus with me also. And I went up by revelation and communicated unto them that gospel which I preach among the Gentiles, but privately to them which were of reputation, lest by any means I should run, or had run, in vain. But neither Titus, who was with me, being a Greek, was compelled to be circumcised: And that because of false brethren unawares brought in, who came in privily to spy out our liberty which we have in Christ Jesus, that they might bring us into bondage: To whom we gave place by subjection, no, not for an hour; that the truth of the gospel might continue with you.'

"Hear Jesus say in Luke 4:18 'The Spirit of the Lord is upon me, because he hath anointed me to preach the gospel to the poor; he hath sent me to heal the brokenhearted, to preach deliverance to the captives, and recovering of sight to the blind, to set at liberty them that are bruised.' To you, former slave, ripped from your homeland, stolen away to this place where you have nobody. God is coming to deliver!"

"Yes, sir. Amen!" the praisers shouted, breathless.

"Let me calm myself and read to you from Galatians the fifth chapter." Allen wiped his brow for the heat had steadily increased within the old smithing shop. When he had regained his breath and steadied himself against the makeshift pulpit, he began to read again.

"'Stand fast therefore in the liberty wherewith Christ hath made us free and be not entangled again with the yoke of bondage. Behold, I Paul say unto you, that if ye be circumcised, Christ shall profit you nothing. For I testify again to every man that is circumcised, that he is a debtor to do the whole law. Christ is become of no effect unto you, whosoever of you are justified by the law; ye are fallen from grace. For we through the Spirit wait for the hope of righteousness by faith. For in Jesus Christ neither circumcision availeth anything, nor uncircumcision; but faith which worketh by love. Ye did run well; who did hinder you that ye should not obey the truth? This persuasion cometh not of him that calleth you. A little leaven leaveneth the whole lump.' Can I get an amen?"

"Amen!" they shouted.

"For all this time, we have worshiped in what we came to know as our place. The white folks resented us taking up their place. They wanted us moved to the back wall of St. George's. Well, here we are in our own Promised Land where it flows with milk and honey."

The floor drumming began again in earnest, and the dancing returned in short order. It would not be quenched.

Allen waited before resuming to preach. "Hear the dictates of the Apostle Paul from the book of Romans. 'Wherefore, my brethren, ye also are become dead to the law by the body of Christ; that ye should be married to another, even to him who is raised from the dead, that we should bring forth fruit unto God. For when we were in the flesh, the motions of sins, which were by the law, did work in our members to bring forth fruit unto death. But now we are delivered from the law, that being dead wherein we were held; that we should serve in newness of spirit, and not in the oldness of the letter.'

"Hear then we will henceforth be known as Bethel—a holy place. We will no longer be moved to the black only spaces. The entire church is a black space. And it's ours. In Romans again, hear God's final pronouncement, 'There is therefore now no condemnation to them which are in Christ Jesus, who walk not after the flesh, but after the Spirit. For the law of the Spirit of life in Christ Jesus hath made me free from the law of sin and death.' The spirit of the Lord is here and where the spirit of the Lord is, there is liberty. And that's Bible."

Chapter 7

CONTROVERSIAL THEOLOGY

I can't, for the life of me, gentlemen, fathom why you have called me to this meeting," said Richard as he addressed the circle of staunch white faces around the large table. The sun strained through the stained-glass windows of St. George's United Methodist Church.

"Well, sir, it involves the stir you and the other negroes caused when you all so loudly walked out of the church during prayer service on Sunday," said an unnamed church trustee.

Raising his eyebrows and sitting back in his chair, Allen pulled at the collar of his suit jacket. "I am sure that was a surprise to the lot of you, but we negroes had our fill of the mistreatment we have felt at your hands."

"Mistreatment? That is laughable," said the overweight gentleman on the opposite side of the table. "We are the only house of worship that has allowed coloreds in the sanctuary. It has been our policy for years."

The other gentlemen agreed, rapping the table and cheering.

"Yes, we have been allowed in the space," said Allen, "but we have never felt free to just be. It's been said that we clap too much, and you don't like when we shout hallelujah in the middle of the sermons as the pastor is speaking. It's said we're either too loud

40

or too excitable. We have put up with your nagging about our expressions of worship." Allen sat forward in his chair and lightly slapped the table. "We even remained quiet and passive when you made us sit in the balcony. We kept our peace, until your welcome didn't feel so welcoming."

The white gentlemen coughed and looked at each other.

"Just imagine what it felt like to be on our knees in prayer after having been ushered upstairs. We had already been seated and were directed to take our seats in the balcony in the colored section. We tried to quietly focus on the goodness of God and not on what it means to be colored in this world." Allen looked at the faces of the men gathered before him, hoping to see some kind of regret. "It was too much, though, when a white man, it may have been you, sir"—Allen pointed at the man seated at the end of the table—"approached my elder friend, Absalom Jones, while his head was bowed in prayer, told him to get up, and intended him to move to the rear of the church."

The elder man Allen had indicated flushed with apparent embarrassment.

"I was within earshot to the whole exchange," said Allen. "I quietly prayed and called out to my God, hoping for a peaceful resolution. I had lifted just lifted my hands in praise when I heard someone tell Absalom, 'You've got to move, boy!' Now, I had told the black saints before that if just one white person says leave him be, we would stay. But not a soul stirred to action that day. Not one welcomed us then. So we left."

Allen stood and started to pace the space behind his chair. "Imagine the ignominy, the disrespect. We were dragged off our knees in this house of the Lord and treated worse than heathens—not with brotherly love nor any shred of human kindness." Allen's tone had now risen to a near shout, his brown face red. "We simply want a place to worship with dignity, not under racial oppression. Is that too much to ask? We didn't mean to cause a ruckus, but we felt disrespected one time too many, so we began our exodus."

When the men before him remained silent, he continued. "I mean, can you imagine what it feels like to worship in this place surrounded by faces in the stained glass—faces that look nothing like your own." Here he ran a hand down his brown cheek. "Then, men who do look like those in the glass saying you don't truly belong? Could it be that these faces"—Allen pointed around the room at the windows—"could it be that these faces don't really reflect to the black people the attitude that they are welcome." He paused to consider the windows, then said. "You know, perhaps Jesus was black."

The men coughed and objected to Allen's depiction of the Christ. "Do not be alarmed at my assertion. The Bible said we are made in his image and likeness. Looking at the brown members of our congregation, it simply makes me think." Allen took his seat.

A fat man to his left, his face red with anger, said, "Surely, Pastor Allen, you are not saying that Jesus was a nig—"

Allen held up his hand. "No, I am not suggesting that. But the Bible does record in the book of Revelation that his hair was like lamb's wool, and he had eyes of fire and feet the color of burnt brass. That is more a far cry from the milky skin of the images we're regularly confronted by," said Allen, pointing again at the windows. "Maybe the artists ran out of colors when they crafted him? Burned brass? That sounds kinda black to me."

"I've heard just about enough of this blasphemer," an angry trustee fumed.

"But why does it matter what Jesus looked like as long as his blood was red?" argued a lay minister. "The images of Jesus as a white man are popular because, let's face it, he was white. And no attempt to darken that image will change the facts. Case closed." He slammed his hand on the table.

"What, pray tell, brings you all such consternation? Surely there is something more than the idea of Jesus's skin color as being something other than white that is causing you to have such difficulty," said Allen. "The Europeanized culture of Jesus has given us a white Jesus regardless of what the Bible says about him. They are designed to make him like y'all. What I will say next is likely to make some of you go mad. If Jesus came to America today, he would likely be a slave."

"Why can't you people just be satisfied with being in the balcony of the church? Why does it always have to be something with you people?" The tall man stood as he argued his point. His beet-red face bespoke his anger and frustration. "Why can't you just stay in your place?"

"Is it the association with Jesus and slavery that bothers you so?" Allen asked, then paused to emphasize his next point. "We will never separate ourselves voluntarily from the slave population in this country. They are our brethren, and we feel there is more virtue in suffering privations with them than a fancied advantage for a season."

Allen wiped his brow of sweat.

"Your objections suggest you do ascribe to the model of white supremacy of Jesus that has been widely accepted. He was a black man, or brown man at the least, from the Middle East," said Allen.

"Brother, Jesus hailed from biblical Israel and was likely white," said another trustee.

"I am not surprised you feel this way," Allen said, sitting back in his chair, enjoying the debate. "I believe the image of Christ has been co-opted, and a white Jesus supports the oppression of my people. We need to liberate people from this image in our collective imagination. My people need to be rescued from this erroneous thinking. There is an amazing freedom in seeing Jesus as you see yourself," Allen said, his hands splayed in from of him. "My parishioners need to see an African Christ setting them free, not an image that has been recycled in the faces of those who hate and despise black bodies. A white Jesus is often used as an implicit or even explicit justification of white dominance," he explained in earnest.

Reverend Pillmore, the pastor, stood and said, "I understand why Brother Allen sees Christ as a negro. People prefer to picture Jesus as looking somewhat like them, or at least like people they are familiar with. The Bible gives no indication of what Jesus looked like. It is a presumption to usurp him as reflecting your own image. Jesus is the Savior for all nations. No matter a person's skin color or race, he can experience forgiveness of sin and reconciliation with God through the crucified and risen Christ. The love of Jesus transcends skin color. Having no physical description of Jesus, people naturally imagine the Son of Man to be like themselves."

Somber now, he lowered his head and looked at the floor.

"Pastor Allen, what happened at church on Sunday was clearly wrong, and I regret it happening. Please apologize to our brethren and tell them they are indeed welcome to return anytime. I am deeply ashamed of our conduct," the elder pastor said.

"Thank you, Reverend. But we must stand against the notion that blacks are incapable of self-governance," said Allen.

"But you took most of our congregants," a white clergyman Allen thought his name was Tom—said. "The church was practically empty when you left."

Allen nodded. "Yes, there were quite a few of us that day. But Absalom and I have started an organization to keep our commitment to help fugitive enslaved peoples fleeing the South who are searching to plant themselves in Philadelphia. And we will be meeting in a church solely for blacks. We will not shrink from our duty. We will not kowtow to white people who wish for our bondage. I made a pledge to God the day I found religion that I would always do the Lord's work."

A trustee on Allen's right huffed out his disgust.

Allen glanced at him but continued. "This I told Rev. Freeborn Garrison, the man who first introduced me to Christ. On that date in September 1779, Rev. Garrison preached to Master Sturgis that weighed in the balance and was found wanting. That message convicted Master Sturgis who surrendered his life to God and then promised freedom for both me and my brother. It is that same spirit calling me to work for our uplift now."

Allen grew quiet momentarily, letting his words sink in. "And that same mission pushes me onward. We will have a home for us to be. Heaven is free for all who worship in spirit and truth." Allen slid his hat from the table "I think this meeting has reached its logical end. I feel we have made no resolution for St. George's, but I have made a resolution for my black brethren. Thank you, gentlemen. I will take my leave now."

Chapter 8

Black Church Challenge

Reverend Allen exited the general store where he had chatted with a church member from the now greatly expanded black church—affectionately known now as "Mother Bethel"—he and Absalom had founded some three years prior.

Together, they had also built and organized the Free African Society, a mutual aid society for free Africans and their descendants who agreed to donate one shilling monthly for the benefit of each other to hand forth to the needy of the society. These free blacks agreed to support one another "in sickness and for the benefit of the widows and fatherless children."

As he made his way down the street, he saw the familiar face of the leader of St. George's.

"Good afternoon, Brother Allen. Can I talk to you for a moment?"

"Yes, Pastor Pillmore, how may I help you?" Allen answered, unsure of what the man wanted. He had not spoken with anyone from St. George's in some years.

"Just wondering if you have gotten this silly black church thing out of your system. I've figured I gave you a few years to try it out. Maybe you want to get in the center of God's will rather than continue playing around the periphery."

"And you are sure of what the Lord's will is for us? How are things at St. George's?" Allen raised the question with a hint of sarcasm.

"Don't get incensed unnecessarily," the elder charmed. "I'm just concerned about you."

"About me? I'm doing the work of the Lord. What gives you concern?"

"I simply do not understand this strange desire to have an all-black church. I thought you balked against segregated worship."

Allen clasped his hands in front of him at his waist, preparing for a new debate. "I do rail against segregation, but what we are not segregated. Your people are welcomed at Bethel. I wish I could say the same about St. George's."

The elder pastor gave Allen a quizzical look. "You were welcome. It was you and your people that chose to leave."

"I see you have forgotten much in the years that have passed. Do you recall we had many conversations about the white congregants being 'uncomfortable' with how my people worshipped? They pushed us to the colored section in the balcony. But even that was not enough for them. They pushed and pushed until we left."

"We could have provided a separate service time for the coloreds."

"And how is that not segregated? How is that welcoming?" Allen shook his head. "Perhaps we left to experience the freedom we have. You should see how great our services have been. I guess it's true what the Bible says in the book of John, 'If the Son sets you free, you will be free indeed.' To see my fellow black brethren experiencing the day of Pentecost every week is something special." Allen pulled at his coat lapel and smiled.

The elder pastor shook his head. "I just do not understand, and I will never understand."

"It is a safe space where we do not have to switch up the way we talk," Allen tried to explain. "We don't need to squelch our desire to praise the Lord in the way we see fit. We are an expressive people, and we need to sometimes be loud, exuberant, boisterous in our praise. At St. George's, we were afraid to say amen or praise the Lord in service because of your lack of comfort. At our church, we can provide my people a respite from the racism they are used to experiencing."

"How does church heal racist experiences, though, if we can't worship together?" asked the elder. "They are just singing a few songs and listening to you preach. There is nothing to get so worked up about. You must be telling them what they want to hear and scratching their itching ears."

"Oh, believe me, they already know about racism. I do not have to speak about racism to scratch that itch," Allen assured him.

The elder tried another tactic to get his point across. "Some of the white mothers were concerned that their young teen daughters were falling prey to the demon of miscegenation. I mean, your people have always been lascivious toward white girls."

"Are you kidding me?" Allen retorted. "I cannot believe you said that."

"You all just worship differently," the man said, switching course again, his face now growing redder and redder. "We are used to having high church, and you all just want us to go back to Africa with your hooting and caterwauling. I sincerely doubt your ability to maintain this scripturally based system of worship. We emphasize plain church and good doctrine. I find it is my job as a Methodist is to evangelize Africa right out of them."

Allen could not believe what he was hearing. The audacity. "Is that all? You just want us to change—to stop being African? But that is who we are, sir. We are descended from Mother Africa."

Pillmore let out a heavy sigh. "I have doubts, Reverend Allen. I wonder if your people are understanding the word we deliver or whether black Christians are even able to interpret religion in the same way that white people can due to their high rate of illiteracy."

Allen tired of the conversation and began looking for a way to end it. He watched people walking by, paying no attention to them. "Most of my people are literate, sir. Many of them educated in Methodist schools—like me."

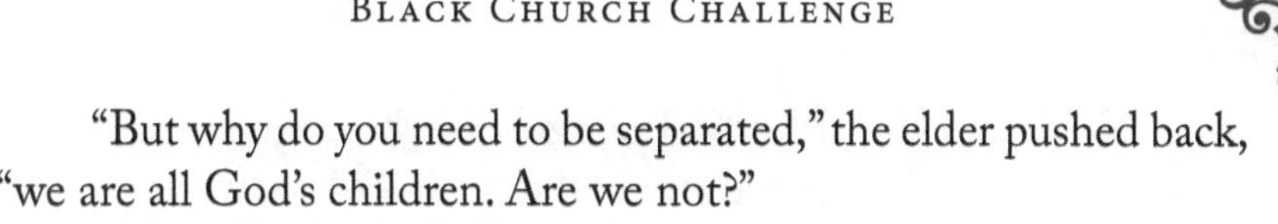

"But why do you need to be separated," the elder pushed back, "we are all God's children. Are we not?"

Allen shot back, "Why can't we have our own space outside of your watching eye?"

The Elder pointed his finger now at Allen. "That question makes me presume you are up to something." He narrowed his eyes. "What are you planning?"

Allen held out his hands. "What would we be planning? I am offended by your assumption."

"Planning or plotting … you know … what do you want to call it?"

The elder had stepped closer to Allen now, and Richard took a step back.

"I do not see your point, nor can I understand why you cannot understand mine."

"Our goal should be uniting the body of Christ," the elder said, once again with his pointer finger. "No matter our color, we are supposed to be one unified people. Just as the Bible calls for—'one Lord, one faith, one baptism.' We are not to be a proponent of racial division."

Allen stepped forward with his own stern look. "Until white people get it and stop terrorizing blacks for being black, there is no unity. You went halfway around the world to make us your slaves and now you want us to come to church together. All you really see is evil. Not the love of God. I cannot, will not bring my people back into that situation. It is bad enough that we must live and breathe and work in this white world." Allen looked at his pocket watch, surprised by the time. "Oh, I really must go. Good day, sir."

Later that day, Richard and his new wife Flora discussed the conversation he'd had with the elder.

"Flora, you will never guess the conversation I had today."

"With whom?" she asked.

"With an elder from St. George's. He harangued me for an hour outside of the general store talking about how we are not in the will of God for being in an all-black church."

"He did not say that. We are not in the will of God?" Flora frowned. "How did he come to that idea?" Flora held the coffee pot strongly in her right hand now, ready to pour into his cup.

Allen held out his cup to her. "He could not see the importance of our group's shared affinity. I think he is feeling the loss of black faces in his congregation. He never recouped after we left."

"That is a shame. That just goes to prove he is not doing any outreach. Philadelphia has so many black people in it."

"He does not comprehend the situation at all. He cannot see the value our group offers for networking, mentorships, and other opportunities. All he sees is a group of black faces potentially plotting against white people. We have got better things to do than plot."

"I hope you told him if white folks would act right, they wouldn't have to worry about us." Flora poured from the coffee pot into her husband's cup then some into her own.

"I did." He stirred cream and sugar into the dark brown liquid and sipped from the cup. "We need each other. Integration is a good thing indeed, but there is something to be said about our being with like kind people."

Flora snorted. "Don't even get me started on the church potlucks. Can we get some seasoning, for goodness sakes? You think they have heard of anything besides salt and pepper? How about some garlic and onion powder."

"Having a black church does so much that is significant to maintain, sustain, buttress, and bolster black people. We do much to support black people needed to support blacks who are racially targeted and criminalized for their political resistance."

"Yes, exactly. I hope you told him that," said Flora as she handed him a cookie from a tray. "He needs to understand that. He needs to know why Bethel exists. We are not exclusive. We exist to be inclusive."

Chapter 9

A Call to Remember
1793–94

The blacks celebrated the development of their own sanctuary but secretly feared white backlash. Debating their choice to walk out of St. George's, Allen confided, "when we hired a storefront and held worship by ourselves, we were pursued with threats of being disowned. We even got subscription papers out to raise money to build the house of the Lord, yet the elder of the Methodist Church still pursued us," Allen defied.

Thinking back on that conversation, the elder had inquired, "Why do you insist on building a black church? I have the charge given to me by the Methodist Conference, and unless you submit, I will read you out publicly of the meeting."

"Show us where we have violated the law," the black preacher shot back, "and then we will submit and seek further redress." His defiance rose in his voice. "We were dragged off our knees in St. George's Church and treated worse than heathens."

Allen continued defending to his other black colleagues, "We were treated thusly in a so-called house of the Lord, and we were determined to seek out for ourselves a true house of worship."

Allen thought back to his conversation with the church leader, "Then you are not Methodists!" He had walked away in a huff.

"He used many arguments to convince us we were wrong in

building a church," Allen reasoned. "He told us to use the funds to raise the glory of St. George's, but it was clear to me, the African Methodists would never return to St. George's."

The church leader had called for a separate meeting with Allen where he continued railing against the building of an African separate church to wit, Allen argued, "If you deny us your name as Methodists, remember, you cannot seal up the scriptures from us, and deny us a name in heaven."

"We will disown you all," the elder threatened.

"While this is a trial I never imagined, I am sure that other Methodists beyond St. George's, including Francis Asbury, will support us," Allen returned, his face consigned in defiant assurance.

For Allen, it was no longer an issue of "if" but "when" they would successfully build.

Sometime in March 1793, Rev. Allen broke ground of the foundation for his planned sanctuary development. He told Absalom, "As I was the first proposer of the African church," he gushed with pride. "I put the first spade in the ground to dig a cellar for that church. Twill be the first African church or meeting house erected in the United States of America."

This groundbreaking paved the way for a new church. It was not to be Allen's Bethel, but his commitment. To the rise of Christendom led his actions.

Absalom wondered, "Should this church be for the Methodists or Episcopalians? I find that many blacks do not want to consider Methodism since St. George's."

Ever the stalwart, Allen pushed for Methodism—"plain and simple." Methodism was the way to convert colored people.

"Too, it was the denomination where I found my freedom in the Lord."

That church would become the St. Thomas's African Episcopal Church, and Absalom accepted the offer to be its head.

By the summer of 1794, Allen would helm the growth and development of the Bethel African Methodist Episcopal Church.

Upon dedicating the property, he announced it "the oldest plot of land to be owned by blacks." The church's official dedication was July 29, 1794. White dignitaries, including Francis Asbury and others, were on hand to lend credence to the fledgling congregation. Asbury delivered the sermon on this important day.

"Our colored brethren are to be governed by the doctrine and discipline of the Methodists," he said. "The AME church will serve as a beacon for saving souls."

Those in attendance shouted their agreement. "Amen!"

When Allen got the opportunity to offer words, he read from Genesis 28:17–19, "And he was afraid, and said, how dreadful is this place! this is none other but the house of God, and this is the gate of heaven. And Jacob rose up early in the morning and took the stone that he had put for his pillows, and set it up for a pillar, and poured oil upon the top of it. And he called the name of that place Bethel…. Bethel marked the place where Jacob saw the gate of heaven and received a manifestation of God."

By 1796, the congregation numbered at least 250 people.

Chapter 10

SECOND THOUGHTS?

"Dear heart, what are you doing?" Flora inquired of her husband's evening activity. "You have been very quiet for some time."

"Getting my sermon ready for tomorrow."

"Oh, what are you going to be talking about?" Flora never asked, but his quietude surprised her. "It must be serious."

Allen hoped his stern look told her volumes of his expectations and need for silence. "I am just very unsettled in my spirit regarding this will of God thing.

"You don't think there is any credence to what the pastor was talking about, do you?"

"Of course not. I have settled that in my heart. But he has me thinking about how to prepare the congregation to challenge those who disparage us. I want them to be ready to give an account and not to be so unsettled a disagreement ensues."

"Well, I leave you be. I'm sure it will be wonderful. Do you need anything? Coffee?"

"No, my dear. I am good, thanks." Allen did not look at his wife as he asked his next question. "Let me ask you, though … what are your thoughts about our decision to leave St. George's?"

"You are asking for my opinion?"

He could hear the surprise in her voice, so he turned to look at her. "Why, yes, you are a valued member of the church. Moreso, you are my wife—an equal partner in the building of Bethel."

Flora held her hand to her throat. "Oh, my. Thank you, husband. I believe … I believe you are letting God lead you as you should, and I am blessed to be your wife."

She gave him a peck on his cheek then exited to the kitchen.

The service had opened much like it always did the following Sunday, with foot stomping, dancing, and washboards. Deacon Jefferson had brought his guitar and picked along, while Allen sat in the pulpit keeping watch over his flock. Despite the boisterous nature of his people, he felt bereft of his usual mirth and folly. When the crowd's expressions of praise died down, Allen stood at the pulpit. "Today," Allen's serious tone suggested the profundity of the morning message, "I want to remind you of where we have come from and why. You may not shout on this one, but you need to hear and listen. Earlier this week, I had a conversation with the pastor of St. George's, and I think he misses us."

Exuberant chuckles burst out among the nearly seventy-five attendees.

"Turn with me to Second Corinthians six seventeen." He read, "'Wherefore come out from among them, and be ye separate, saith the Lord, and touch not the unclean thing; and I will receive you.' Some people do not understand why we left. Some people do not understand why we want an all-black church."

"Yeah, some white people," a singular unidentified male voice spoke from the rear.

Another voice echoed "You got that right" amid laughs.

Allen chuckled under his breath. "In all seriousness, if someone raised this question to you of why you need an all-black church and perhaps questions the will of God regarding our Bethel, I want you to be prepared for this occurrence. It is going to happen."

He let the murmurs die down before talking again.

"In the text today, the Apostle Paul tells the Corinthian Christians to set strong boundaries for themselves when it relates to non-Christian threats. He strongly told them to 'come from among them and be separate.'

"Some of you remember Exodus Sunday when we walked out of service at St. George's. You could say this was our way of staying true to this teaching considering the unchristian conduct of them violating colored folks."

A female voice agreed with a loud, "Yessir."

"You remember, Sister Johnson? You were there." Allen remembered his compatriots of that fateful day in 1787. "We considered it our duty to devise a plan in order to build a house of our own, to worship God under our own vine and fig tree."

"Amen, brother," Sister Johnson said as she rocked in her pew, her hand on her chest.

Allen continued, "For the last couple of years, we have been enjoying our time in the shade of our own tree and our Methodist brothers disagree. They consider us outcasts while seeing themselves as the children of God. The Bible tells us to 'watch and pray' and to 'know them that labor among you' and to set boundaries around your heart. I wish to tell you God is not displeased with our worship. He is displeased with the reason why our worship is the way it is. Our separation should be laid at the feet of our white brothers who refuse to be near us and for those who consider our presence a nuisance and seek to push us back or away. I am here to tell you God is not pleased."

"Say that!" a male voice chimed in.

"We are not immune from the discrimination our colored brothers and sisters experience. We are in this world and not of this world. We must not sink to hatred like the children of Israel in the Old Testament. In due time, our oppressors will be punished. But now hear me when I say this, only God has the right to judge their sin. And it is true that God is slow to anger, and you may feel righteous in your indignation toward them for the way they have treated us, but God's voice prompts us to forgive them and show them love, regardless of the situation."

Allen concluded with a call for nationwide repentance that God would both heal and forgive the racism of the land and its people. He implored those in attendance to both hear and obey so as not to incur God's disappointment. After he had offered up the closing prayer, he looked down at his wife seated on the front pew. She smiled, her eyes sparkling.

Chapter 11

Yellow Fever Epidemic
1793

Absalom, let me read what we have so far." Allen read from his notepad. "We have many unprovoked enemies, who begrudge us the liberty we enjoy, and are glad to hear of any complaint against our color, be it just or unjust; in consequence of which we are more earnestly endeavoring all in our power to warn, rebuke and exhort our African friends, to keep a conscience void of offense towards God and man; and, at the same time, would not be backward to interfere, when stigmas or oppression appear pointed at, or attempted against them, unjustly, and we are confident … and we are confident …" He paused a moment, tapping his pencil on the paper. "What do we want to say here?"

They had decided to write and publish "A Narrative of the Proceedings of Black People During the Awful Calamity in Philadelphia in the Year 1793" in answer to the racist attack by Matthew Carey who had charged black people with profiting from the recent yellow fever outbreak.

Absalom looked over his shoulder at the words they'd written. "And we are confident we shall stand justified in the sight of the candid and judicious for such conduct."

Allen repeated Jones' words to himself. "Yes, that sounds good. And we need to up our publication strategy. It is the wave of the future. It is the way to protest. We will be like Prince Hall, William Hamilton, or Olaudah Equiano—every one of these figures have produced pamphlets of protest. Printed publications make our plight visible and seen by our detractors. They cannot ignore the printed word," he said.

Absalom wondered aloud, "If we take this position, will it weaken our cause among our white brethren? Those who are allies, I should say."

Allen shook his head. "I do not think so. The pastor has alleged I am racist against white people, but I told him white people are welcome at Bethel. He won't believe me, though. I will need to hire some white boy and move him into my house to prove I am pro-integration, I suppose."

"You might be right." Absalom rubbed his chin as he paced about the room. "Hey, what about that boy, Nichola Fulkers? I hear he is looking for a place to live. He has been looking for a relatively cheap place to rent."

Allen nodded. "I think I will ask him to move in. The pastor won't be accusing me of engendering a black enclave around the neighborhood. I can integrate," Allen said.

"Unrelated to our article," Absalom said. "The coffers are low. We are going to need to get some funds up to keep making repairs at the church. We are attracting a larger share of the free blacks in the region, and they are not the farmhands you've been used to."

"I will talk to Brother Benjamin Rush to possibly secure a loan from the Pennsylvania Abolition Society. What do you say … fifty pounds? We should also branch out—buy that nail factory we've previously discussed. The construction business is booming, and we need to get into that fray. I will even put my home up as collateral to help fund it. Interested? You can be my partner. We will call it Absalom Jones and Company as you are the elder of us. It is only natural to name it after you. I will be Company," said Allen.

"We will need a few young men to learn the trade. We'll have to get them to learn how to manufacture nails," said Absalom.

"Yes, and I will provide their shelter and provide food, and we'll have to pay their freedom dues."

"Don't you need to run all this by Flora?" Absalom considered Allen's wife.

"I will. I am confident of her support though."

Their business venture started later that summer of 1793 with a substantial loan from the abolitionists. The business proved to be a boon for the black community, built on the credible name of Richard Allen.

But it all came to a sudden and screeching halt when yellow fever broke out in Philadelphia in the late summer.

"Allen, what are we going to do? The city is a ghost town," Jones lamented one day. "Look over there. All those homes are boarded up and empty. It's as if terror has now become universal."

Richard quoted scripture to him. "'The Lord is my light and my salvation, whom shall, I fear? The Lord is the strength of my life. Of whom shall I be afraid?'"

Jones faltered a moment. "Scripture is fine, but people are dying and there is disease everywhere. They're banning businesses from sending goods and people from Philadelphia."

"I only know the power of God's word. Psalms 91 tells us 'Thou shalt not be afraid for the terror by night; nor for the arrow that flieth by day; Nor for the pestilence that walketh in darkness; nor for the destruction that wasteth at noonday,'" Allen said confidently.

"But …" Absalom waxed timid. His concern showed on his face.

"'A thousand shall fall at thy side, and ten thousand at thy right hand; but it shall not come nigh thee.'" Allen quoted.

Despite his persistence to fight the good fight, Allen fell ill in September and was hospitalized until mid-November. Thankfully, his resources were able to shore up his family during that time.

One sunny afternoon in September, Flora inquired how he was feeling.

"I have chills, pains in my chest, and a splitting headache," he told her from his hospital bed, "but God has me in the palm of his hand. Do not worry, dear heart. There are so many worse off than me. Some patients lost their reason and raged with the fury madness could produce. Thank God for good doctors like Benjamin Rush. He gave me laudanum, and they are taking good care of me."

The effects of yellow fever ravaged the city. Businesses shuttered and people died. They could not locate a cause, but physician Benjamin Rush believed blacks were immune because they did not get sick during the first wave of the disease. By the time Richard was released on November 20, Rush had conscripted his help to visit the abodes of wretchedness, to enter the feelings of the unfortunate, to sympathize with their sorrows and relieve their distresses.

"Surely," he told Allen, "these actions are truly elevating and ennobling above the rest of mankind. This fever infects white people of all ranks but passes by persons of your color. You are under no obligation to me for being a part of your healing save to tend to your own flock, but I hope pleasing in the light of that God who will see every act of kindness done to creatures whom he calls his brethren as if done to himself."

"Alright, Doctor, I'll do it," Allen said.

"How could you agree to that, Richard Allen? It is like walking into a death trap. You are just getting out of the hospital yourself," Flora, his wife, stated out of concern, standing with her hands on her hips when he'd told her of his agreement with Rush.

"Flora, it is the only way to mend the fences with the white folks who are still twisted about our exodus from St. George's. This will get us back in their good graces. Not to mention how the white abolitionists have been good to the blacks. They have secured loans for us and provided legal aid for runaway slaves. The Free African Society can pitch in as nurses to attend to the afflicted. It is our civic duty. And together, we blacks and whites will work to solve a public health crisis and somehow maintain civil order," Richard said.

"If you think so, I will commit," Flora agreed.

They first called upon a family where the father had been afflicted. Allen, accompanied by Absalom Jones, nursed the man back to health by providing chicken soup Flora had made. When the man recovered, they were buoyed by their good work. Allen felt comforted in the fact the black workers were being of use to the white people and felt good they were not being thought of as black slaves, but citizens trying to do public good.

"This is terrible work, Richard," Absalom complained one day as they tended in another sick person's abode.

"A true statement indeed," Allen agreed. "It is uncommon to find anyone that would go near, much more handle, a sick or dead person. But the black community volunteers have worked to dig graves to bury the dead and to bury bed linens and clothes as well. Caring for the sick and dying is not without challenges,"

"Oh, my goodness, I had to grab this one white man who flailed about. He did not want me to touch him, the fever made him mad. I know we were encouraged not to touch them, but when he ran away—what else could I do?" Absalom asked.

Similar stories abounded of tales of those tormented by the disease.

A black nurse chimed in her experience. "That was nothing. I went into one house and the lady was lying on the floor stark naked and covered in blood."

Allen nodded. "Yes, I know it has been difficult, but you are doing good work. It shatters the wall between blacks and whites." Allen's stoic nature helped him ignore the emotional responses.

The next day, Allen pushed his death cart down the street, calling, "Bring out your dead!" He had already accumulated several corpses for his wagon. Soon, he heard a woman's voice yelling for help.

"Over here!" She waved to get his attention. "Inside, he's inside. It's my husband!" the woman yelled as she feverishly pointed for Allen and his team to come inside the house.

When they entered, their nostrils were assaulted by a foul

aroma. Allen knew immediately the smell of rotting and decaying flesh—especially after pushing the cart around all day.

"When did he pass away, ma'am?"

"It's been several days now," she confided, wringing her hands into a handkerchief. "I didn't want to call for help. I was fearful of losing him, but the smell is so awful now."

"Not to worry, madam. We'll take care of the body for you. Have you planned with a local mortician? Or should I just take him to the mass grave?" Allen asked.

"I have not. I will do that today. Oh, thank you, sir. Your kindness to me is laudatory," she said.

He called out to those who were assisting, "Alright, you grab his legs, and we'll carry him to the wagon."

A black nurse was standing near admiring a golden candlestick setting on the table.

"Don't you touch that. It is a priceless heirloom," the woman sternly chastised her.

Stunned, the black woman raised her hands in the air. "I was just looking at it, ma'am. It is terribly pretty."

"You were trying to steal from me," the white woman accused, her good nature now gone.

The black woman's eyes grew wide. "No, ma'am, that's just not true."

"We will just be on our way, then. No harm," Allen said, ushering his volunteers out with the body.

The following week, there rose a story in the local press alleging the black volunteers had been stealing from the white citizens. This story awakened much of white persons' racial fears. A reporter approached Reverend Allen about the charges.

"This is complete nonsense, and I don't believe it at all," he told the reporter. "We are just doing a public service. The Bible says in Romans 14 'Let not then your good be evil spoken of.' I will inform my workers about that very thing. We will not accept the blame for this."

Chapter 12

GRIEVANCES

I just want to stand and thank so many of you for assisting us this week as we have pledged to rid the city of the aftermath of the plague," Allen told his congregation the following Sunday. "I know it has not been easy work. In fact, it was quite scary. The doctors don't really have an idea of where it came from, and much information has gone out about how it spreads. We have been afraid to encounter others and have come close to the dead."

"Sure did, Pastor," said a black nurse from the front pew.

"Some of you may have lingering concerns about your own health, but I want to encourage you to trust in God," Allen reassured. "My text today comes from the book of Proverbs, chapter three, verses five through ten. Turn there if you will."

He waited before reading.

"'Trust in the Lord with all thine heart; and lean not unto thine own understanding. In all thy ways acknowledge him, and he shall direct thy paths. Be not wise in thine own eyes: fear the Lord and depart from evil. It shall be health to thy navel, and marrow to thy bones. Honour the Lord with thy substance, and with the first fruits of all thine increase: So shall thy barns be filled with plenty, and thy presses shall burst out with new wine.'

"Trusting in God is a very common theme throughout the Bible. Psalm 37:3 tells us to 'Trust in the Lord and do good; so shalt thou dwell in the land, and verily thou shalt be fed.' Psalm 37:5 says 'Commit thy way unto the Lord; trust also in him; and he shall bring it to pass.' Trust means to lie helpless, face down in complete submission—like a servant waiting for his Master's command. The focus of trust is submission," Reverend Allen said.

Voices of agreement poured from the audience.

Allen continued. "Lean on him refers to the custom of leaning to the left at Passover. It is a custom to take a pillow with you for the meal and lean on it while eating, reminding you that you must always lean on God; it is not by our own might or power, but by his Spirit. Acknowledge him, invite him into Lordship in all your life. Make your paths straight. This is his will for your life, not yours. Fear him but not to be afraid, but to revere him, his wisdom and ways."

"Yes sir," a voice called out from the congregation.

"When the Bible tells us in this verse not to lean on our own understanding, it is not encouraging us to be irrational. The Bible puts up no wall of separation between our intellect and faith. In fact, the book of Proverbs speaks very highly of understanding. It says to 'Incline your heart to understanding' in Proverbs 2:2. Let me list some other scriptures for you. Write these down so you can study them later."

He waited until they had taken out their notebooks or found slips of paper to use.

"Proverbs 2:6 says understanding will guard you. Proverbs 3:12 reminds us that blessed is the one who gets understanding. Proverbs 16:16 says having wisdom is better than gold and silver, and Proverbs 23:23 tells us to buy wisdom, instruction, and understanding, but do not sell it.

"So, if we're supposed to get understanding, why are we not supposed to lean on it?" Allen held up his finger. "We're told not to lean on our own understanding or make conclusions based primarily on our own perceptions. Our own understanding simply will not bear the full weight of reality," said Allen.

"Alright now," Sister Hubbard rang in.

"In Eden, Adam and Eve were forbidden to eat from the tree of the knowledge of good and evil and were not refused the tree of life. It was not life that God denied human beings. He simply wanted them to trust in him completely, but he still gave them the freedom of their own will. He wants us to trust in him, but he gives us the ability to decide to do it on our own. The point of this prohibition was not to keep humans ignorant but, as John Piper says, 'to preserve the pleasures of the world' that God had created for them." It was as if God was saying, 'If you eat of that one tree you will be saying to me 'I'm smarter than you, I am more authoritative than you, I am wiser than you are, I think I can care for myself better than you care for me, you are not a very good father, and so, I am going to reject you.'"

A few murmurs came from his congregation. They knew how harsh these things would be to say to the Lord.

"So don't eat from the tree, because you will be rejecting me and all my good gifts and all my wisdom and all my care. Instead, keep on submitting to my will, keep on affirming my wisdom, keep on being thankful for my generosity, keep on trusting me as a father, and keep on eating from these other trees as a way of enjoying me."

Allen wiped his forehead free of sweat with a handkerchief. "To handle the knowledge of good and evil, one must possess the ability to completely comprehend all possible options, which is omniscience, the righteousness and wisdom to choose the right course, and the power to make reality conform to the right course, omnipotence. Only God can handle such knowledge."

"Amen, pastor!"

"Trusting in the Lord is not irrational, but trusting in yourself and your own abilities is. It is insane to trust such pitifully limited understanding when one can trust the unlimited understanding of God.

"So many of the things that cause us the most difficulty and heartache in life, the source of so much of our anxiety, fear, doubt, and anger with others and with God, is the result of leaning on our own understanding. God does not want us to be miserable. He wants to relieve our anxiety, fear, doubt, and sinful anger. And so, he gives us Proverbs 3:5–6 as a priceless gift."

Allen paced as he talked. "You need to start exercising faith by trusting fully in the Lord and not leaning on our own understanding. We're not setting aside the knowledge God has given us. We're submitting our understanding to the intellect of God. It is the wisest and most sane thing we can do. It will ultimately lead to joy, even with our journey full of sorrowful experiences. Will you submit your life to him? Will you trust in him with all your heart?"

The room had grown quiet now as each parishioner contemplating his words.

"Let me close by reading James 4:1–8. 'From whence come wars and fightings among you? come they not hence, even of your lusts that war in your members? Ye lust, and have not: ye kill, and desire to have, and cannot obtain: ye fight and war, yet ye have not, because ye ask not. Ye ask, and receive not, because ye ask amiss, that ye may consume it upon your lusts. Ye adulterers and adulteresses, know ye not that the friendship of the world is enmity with God? whosoever therefore will be a friend of the world is the enemy of God. Do ye think that the scripture saith in vain, The spirit that dwelleth in us lusteth to envy? But he giveth more grace. Wherefore he saith, God resisteth the proud, but giveth grace unto the humble. Submit yourselves therefore to God. Resist the devil, and he will flee from you. Draw nigh to God, and he will draw nigh to you. Cleanse your hands, ye sinners; and purify your hearts, ye double minded.'" A small number of congregants stood and clapped their hands.

"I choose to trust in God—not the naysayers whose focus is on the pestilence. I'm going back out this week, and I'm going to keep doing the right thing. Stand to your feet and let's pray.

"Savior, your word declares in Psalm 91 that you would 'deliver us from the snare of the fowler, and from the noisome pestilence.' Protect us from this disease that is going around, and we ask that you deliver Philadelphia from this curse it has fallen under. In the name of Jesus, Amen."

Absalom Jones shared his thoughts with Allen after the service. "While I appreciate what you preached today, my friend, there is more to fear than pestilence. No matter what we do, we still get blamed. If something turns up missing, the black people must have stolen it, right? We are a lightning rod for nonsense."

"I know, I know," Allen returned, "It seems that way. The newspapers are reporting racial divisiveness. Even our nurses are getting blamed."

"We feel ourselves sensibly aggrieved by the censorious epithets of many who did not render the least assistance in the time of necessity. They did not even lift a finger. Leave it for the colored folk. Even to this day, it is generally received opinion in the city that our color was not so liable to the sickness as the whites," Jones said.

"Yes, that is correct. I fear this will continue as the numbers of black people grow amid white folks fleeing Philadelphia. Black numbers are growing and becoming more evident. I fear that some white folks will aim to reinstitute slavery because of our numbers growing. Did you read the latest *Gazette* with the conversation between two farmers from New Jersey? They fear us. It is akin to modern day Egypt when the Egyptians feared the numbers of Israelite slaves and wanted to clamp down on their growth."

"Terrible." Absalom shook his head. "Lord, forbid we get paid like those white tradesmen do for our work, especially our nurses. White folks do not dare to even get near to yellow fever victims."

A disgruntled Jones continued to rant. "And how about the mayor adding fuel to the fire when he said, 'The people who are employed to remove the dead?' Employed, *hmpf*. I wish they would pay us like employees. We have been frequently interrupted, insulted, and threatened by those who appear to possess no sentiment of humanity. I would appreciate a tittle of the recognition he lavishes on the white helpers."

"Now, remember"—Allen tapped his friend on the shoulder—"we are not working for money or recognition. The mayor referred to white folks as 'citizens' and us coloreds as 'useful persons.' When do you think blacks will ever earn the respect they deserve."

"And still, we contend with this nonsense that Matthew Carey is pushing through his pamphlet. He says that groups of 'the vilest blacks' are roaming city streets, causing trouble, and ripping off 'helpless' whites." Absalom laughed. "He recklessly charged some of them —meaning us blacks—with being detected of plundering and ransacking abandoned white homes and attacking weakened whites over their purses without one shred of evidence."

"He doesn't have to," Allen said. "Carey is playing on racial fears. All he must do is amplify the notion that blacks are on the loose like we have escaped the circus. Whatever to stoke white folks predisposed thinking."

"His words will prejudice the minds of the people in general against us. Suppose one of our volunteers is unfairly suspected and implicated when trying to do their job? White citizens will assume that all blacks belong to the vilest class," Jones returned.

Allen nodded. "That is it. You and I should write an essay to counter this narrative. We should publish it ourselves. Why should we allow the white voice to rule? Our people deserve us to be loud and tell the truth."

"But Carey's accusations have been read by hundreds … thousands. It is in the third printing. Even if we were able to capture every black reader in Philadelphia, 'An ill name is easier given than taken away,'" Jones expressed.

"We won't worry about that. I just want to make him take his words back to the pit of Hades," said Allen.

Chapter 13

EPIDEMIC COSTS
1793–94

Of a truth, Richard, the epidemic has cost us money for real," Absalom said one day. "I fear we are in dire straits. We have dedicated some seventy days to yellow fever clean up. I mean, between the two of us, we have worked a full two months with no break."

"Well, you were working that time. I was laid up in the hospital from September to November. You were out here breaking your back."

"You weren't there physically, but you were there," Jones expressed.

"I can say it was costly work. We had to rent carriages to carry the dead bodies and we hired five assistants to bury the beds of the infected. Sum total, after all that, we have expended some one hundred seventy-eight pounds."

Absalom shook his head. "You and I will need to get busy to recoup our losses then."

"Not just us personally, but the nail factory too."

"Yes, I hadn't even thought about how slow business had been throughout the epidemic," Absalom complained. "Have you been able to make your payment on the loan to the Abolition Society? You don't want to be bound over to the debtor's prison. That would not be good for your name at all. Nor if you let your house be taken away. That would be an expensive cost for coffins and hearses, indeed. If only we had been paid or reimbursed for our fever work."

"Truer words have never been spoken, sir," Allen confirmed. "I say we visit the Pennsylvania Abolition Society and explain our situation. Perhaps they will understand?"

"Yes, we can explain the loss sustained on account of our services during the late sickness in the city. They should understand," Jones agreed.

"We can have them review our books and expenditures. We have nothing to hide."

The duo met twice with the Pennsylvania Abolitionist Society first to explain the hardship left by the yellow fever epidemic and a second time to let the organization review their financials. The PAS were concerned with the condition of the morals of free Negroes and Jones' and Allen's superintendency.

"Sir, I assure you," Jones implored during their second meeting, "We have made no money during this time. We have spent this money in support of the city. Reverend Allen and I have served as nurses to try to increase the health of those within the city to the great loss of ourselves. Perhaps you can consider forgiving the loan?"

"Reverend Jones, both you and Reverend Allen have been exemplary stewards of the colored remnant in Philadelphia," a white abolitionist of the organization affirmed, "but I am afraid, the loan must be repaid."

He would make no special consideration. Yet, he understood the hardship and agreed to offer an essay—of sorts—to support Jones and Allen and confirm their financial position.

After nearly two weeks, the gentlemen received the essay decision by mail. Allen read the essay aloud to his friend. The document confirmed Jones and Allen as "sufferers" of the epidemic in relief of the sick and internment of the dead during the prevalence of the fever in 1793 and the Pennsylvania Abolitionists Society identified as the "whole losers" should the loan not be fully repaid.

Allen folded the letter and breathed a sigh. "It was just like I expected. We have lost money because of the people who refused to pay for our work to aid." He attempted to appear comforted, but he felt his forehead crease with concern. He smacked the letter against his thigh. "We will publish an essay in response. Clearly, racism is part of this answer. How can our case be considered in any other way when white folks have less to defend? The Society will undoubtedly be inundated with many requests from blacks. How can they keep taking funds from black educational endeavors and respond with this? I am determined to pay off this debt now more than ever."

"'We do not wish to make you angry,'" Allen read from the essay they'd been working on, "'but excite your attention to consider how hateful slavery is in the sight of God, who hath destroyed kings and princes for their oppression of the poor slaves.'"

"Yes, that says it," Jones supported. "We must let the so-called Christians know they should fear God's wrath and divine punishment."

Allen nodded. "I'm tired of sugarcoating. They do not need moralism or platitudes. They need to understand the fear of God. I will be an instrument of righteousness and plead the cause of the oppressed."

"Yes, sir, I will too."

"This essay is timely as the federal government has just adopted a fugitive slave law and there is a flood of former slaves from Haiti finding rescue in Philadelphia. We must strike while the iron is hot. There is much antislavery talk, revolutionary activity, and slaveholder concern about bondage. We must propel the black abolitionist voice against bondage and racial injustice. These gradual abolition laws are not enough."

"No, they are not. 'Tis a true statement indeed," Jones agreed. "Of a truth, no Southern state will ever pass a gradual emancipation law."

"It is a true statement, but if they love their children, love their country, even love the God of love," Allen declared, "then clear their hands from slaves, and burden not their children or country with them."

"Amen, preacher."

"Abolition now, not gradually. Abolition is the only way to save the country safely and practically. If they truly want to be known as a patriot, they need to set the black people free. It is the slaveholders' conundrum—to call yourselves a country conceived in liberty on the backs of my black brothers."

"That's a powerful statement," Absalom said.

"I remember reading Benjamin Banneker's almanac last year, printed in 1793. He really captured my defense against Jefferson's comments on slavery. Jefferson said, 'The whole commerce between master and slave is a perpetual exercise of the most boisterous passions, the most unremitting despotism on the one part, and degrading submissions on the other. Our children see this' Jefferson admitted, 'and learn to imitate it.' That's true. I remember Master Chew's young boy—he played like he was my friend one day and the next day he called me a nigger to my face."

"No, he did not, surely," Absalom asked. "That must have smacked you in the face."

"For sure. Jefferson had the audacity to say liberty was the gift of God. He so much as shared a hatred of slavery but had yet to set his own slaves free." Allen's forehead wrinkled in anger as he considered Jefferson's words. "They worried that having a country of free-roaming blacks loose on the towns would be detrimental to their lily-white society. I tell you if they would just give us a free education and treat us equally, there would not be a worry. As we have seen, blacks only want what white folks want—to be left alone and to prove nothing to anybody. We want to raise our children and not have to beat away bigots. To be useful, not to be a slave just for being black. If you leave people mired in educational and social wastelands, and they will sink to the level of expectation." Allen's chest swelled with racial pride.

"It's so very true."

"The slave master has been told to liberate the slave, and I have said to the liberated blacks at Bethel that God calls them to love their former masters for the scriptures have called us to 'love our enemies, to do good to them that hate and despitefully use us.' Our freedom does not equal danger to them in the least."

"That should resonate beyond slaveholders. Think of the Abolitionist Society, they distribute pamphlets showing such obvious paternalism—the guarantors or guardians of freedom, the moral overseers. They look at us as simple machines and brute animals. White folks have mastered art, science, and literature, and we poor deviant blacks need to be rescued."

Jones was so frustrated he broke into a sweat. He tugged at his waist coat to ensure his neatness.

Chapter 14

Living Nativity

The singing had quieted, and the drumming had slowed, and Allen approached the podium in his classic black suit jacket.

"Today, I'm going to do something out of the ordinary. You kids come on up and sit next to me. James, Xavier, Adell. Children ages four through eleven, come join me. I want to talk to you. Parents, you have the morning off. I just want to preach to the kids."

Allen waited while the children ran to the front of the church. He knelt and got on their level with a grunt.

"Today, boys and girls, I am going to point out some things from the Christmas story in Luke the second chapter. Let me read from verse seven." He opened his Bible and began to read. "'And she brought forth her firstborn son, and wrapped him in swaddling clothes, and laid him in a manger; because there was no room for them in the inn.'

"Joseph and Mary were about to have a new baby! Remember when your baby brother was coming, Jill? Wasn't that exciting?" He smiled at the children watching him with rapt attention. "This was Mary and Joseph's first baby, and his birth had been prophesied to them by an angel. The angel told them this baby would be the Messiah for Israel and the whole world!"

Just then, the door opened wide and Brother Hubbard entered, leading his wife on a donkey. A few of the children giggled at the large bump Sister Hubbard grasped around her waist indicating she was pregnant. One young boy reached out to pet the donkey's muzzle.

Once the kids' marveling had ceased, Rev. Allen continued. "The city of Bethlehem was full of travelers during that time. All the places in town were so packed there were no rooms available for them. Joseph finally found one lowly place where they could bunk. Mary's time was close."

Sister Hubbard grabbed at her belly and exhaled aloud. "Joseph, I think it's time!" She winced.

Brother Hubbard, dressed as Joseph, accepted his wife's hand and helped her dismount the beast. "It's a good thing this inn gave us space, even though it's a manger with farm animals. At least we have a place to stay. Let's get you settled and then I'll go find a midwife." Brother Hubbard helped his wife to the floor and rushed out of the scene.

Reverend Allen broke into the scene. "Joseph and Mary had to travel from their hometown of Nazareth a long way to the town of their ancestors' birth, Bethlehem in Judea. They did this because the Roman emperor had demanded that everyone pay taxes and that a census be taken to count all the people in the kingdom. It didn't take very long before Mary started having childbirth pains and finally Jesus was born. There was no room for him, but God made a way!"

Sister Hubbard now cuddled her newborn child—just a doll wrapped up to look like a baby—and kissed his face.

"God will always make a way in your life even when people don't welcome you into their lives," Allen continued. "The Bible says that God will never forsake you and that He will be with you always even until the end of time. Although there was no room for Jesus and He had to be born in a stable, He has made room for you today! You have a place to lay your head, you have God's guardian angels around you, and you are protected by the power of God in Christ. There is always a place for you in the kingdom of God!"

Allen paused a moment for his words to sink in for the children.

"Jesus came as a baby, and they put him in a manger." Allen told the kids. "Mangers are what we put hay and grain in for animals to eat. Even though He is the King of Kings, his birth was very humble … just like our birth. If a king can be born in a stable and laid in a manger, then think of what God can do for you! You are bound to be free! You are children of the highest. Though you may have been born in humble circumstances, you will reign in the Kingdom of God."

Several of the children smiled, still enraptured by the story.

"Mary snuggled her new baby," Allen continued as Sister Hubbard rocked and cooed the doll in her arms. "He was wrapped in swaddling clothes, which are the blankets used to wrap newborn animals in, to keep them warm. God wraps us in His arms and gives us the security of His love in the same way. He not only brings you into his Kingdom as dear children, but he wraps you up in his love, mercy, and grace. You never have to feel alone anymore. God himself is with you. He is with you! Repeat after me, children … He is for me."

All the children repeated enthusiastically, "He is for me!"

Reverend Allen smiled. "Yes. He loves you. He has made a place for you in His Kingdom."

Several men dressed as shepherds entered the barn. One pulled a small sheep behind him.

"Somehow word got out and soon some shepherds came to see little baby Jesus," Allen said.

One shepherd spoke to Sister Hubbard as Mary, "Is this the Expected One?"

She did not answer but only lifted the baby for the shepherd to see him better.

Another shepherd said, "An angel appeared to us on the hill. We were all afraid. That is until he told us 'Do not fear.' I expected to die. Still, he pressed on with his announcement. He told us 'Behold, I bring you good tidings of great joy, which shall be to all people. For unto you is born this day in the city of David a Savior, which is Christ the Lord. And this shall be a sign unto you; Ye shall find the babe wrapped in swaddling clothes, lying in a manger.' And here he is."

Brother and Sister Hubbard, dressed as Mary and Joseph, held tightly to their son as the shepherds told their tale.

The youngest shepherd pushed the first. "Don't forget the angelic choir."

"Oh, yes … Suddenly, the skies were filled by angels. They sang 'Glory to God in the highest. Peace on Earth to men of Good Will.' It was amazing and glorious to behold. We rushed to find the child and praised the Lord the whole way. Now, we have found him."

"It wasn't long before this group had been joined by three men—clearly foreigners," Allen narrated.

The wise men entered, each one bearing a gift to present to the Christ child.

"We have traveled from afar," said the tallest man. "We've been following his star. We knew it would lead us here. Now that we have found him, we each want to give the child a gift. I have brought him gold. Gold, fit for a king. We will hail him as the 'King of the Jews.' Caspar, what have you brought to the king?"

"I have brought frankincense, a sweet-smelling oil to represent his divinity." Caspar nodded toward Joseph as if to indicate he understood the unique place the man held as the child's father. "What have you brought Balthazar?"

"I have brought myrrh." He presented his gift and knelt in reverence. "May it please you, O King."

Allen turned back to the children to conclude the story. "These are not the usual gifts you bring to a new baby, but their gifts were useful, respectful, and precious. Some of the best gifts we can give the Savior are our time and talents, which we can use in the service of others. The gifts the wise men brought were the kinds of gifts they would have brought to a king. Jesus Christ is indeed our king—and much more. May we give generously to Him, as He has so abundantly given to us, by living and loving as He has so patiently taught. The wise men had searched for Jesus for at least ten days. And let me tell you, wise men still seek him today."

The program concluded with all the participants bowing before the Christ family.

Reverend Allen clapped his hands and declared, "Merry Christmas to all of God's children!" He stood with hands raised, praying, "Heavenly Father, thank you for your Son born to a world that would treat him so unkindly. May we all daily bring you our gifts and surrender them to you as we serve you. We each pledge to use our time and talents in your service, and we will forever glorify you. Bless these children and help them to grow up to serve you. In Jesus' name, amen."

Just as Pastor Allen finished praying, the sheep began defecating. The children collectively cried out and pointed, "Ewww!" James added, "He's pooping. That's so nasty!"

Allen could not resist the opportunity to make this a spiritually appropriate moment. "Well, it's not nasty, but that's just what Jesus does. He cleans up the messes we make. Deacon, will you clean that up, please?"

Chapter 15

An Elegy for a President
1799

Rising, Pastor Allen in black cleric's gown carried his Bible to the platform. "It is with great sadness that I rise today and must inform you of the recent death of the General—President George Washington—who has shuffled off this mortal coil and returned to the Lord our Creator."

A few parishioners gasped at the news.

"What? I hadn't heard," cried Sister Myrtle.

"At this time, it may not be improper to speak a little on the late mournful event—an event in which we participate in common with the feelings of a grateful people—an event which causes the land to mourn in a season of festivity. We have just experienced a celebration of the mass unto Christ, but our father and friend has been taken from us—he whom the nations honored is seen of men no more. It may be confusing to some of you that I consider this a sad occasion for it is true that Washington was a slaveowner. And while I do not mourn his loss, it is a terrible day for this country as it has lost its first leader," Allen said.

"Amen," a brother in black suit agreed.

"We, my friends, have particular cause to bemoan our loss. To us he has been the sympathizing friend and tender father. He has watched over us and viewed our degraded and afflicted state with compassion and pity. His heart was not insensible to our sufferings. He whose wisdom the nations revered thought we had a right to liberty. Unbiased by the popular opinion of the state in which is the memorable Mount Vernon, he dared to do his duty and wipe off the only stain with which man could ever reproach him," Allen said.

"Honestly, Pastor, a slaveowner he was. Why should we care about this slaveowner's death?" a large black woman spoke out loud.

"Right. Right," another agreed nodding her head.

"It's true, but what many of you didn't know, Washington supported our cause at Bethel. He gave us money to start our very own church as he recognized the need for us to have a designated place to attend church. And it is now said by an authority on which I rely, that he who ventured his life in battles, whose head was covered in that day, and whose shield the Lord of hosts was, did not fight for that liberty which he desired to withhold from others—the bread of oppression was not sweet to his taste, and he let the oppressed go free. He undid every burden—he provided lands and comfortable accommodations for them when he kept this acceptable fast to the Lord—that those who had been slaves might rejoice in the day of their deliverance."

"Yes, sir," a black-suited, well-dressed man yelled from the back.

"I had occasion to talk with slaves who had run away from Washington's Mount Vernon in Virginia. Just two months ago, Ona Judge, his wife's seamstress and body servant, had patronized the shoe store at my house. A lovely woman. Dressed real fancy. A light, freckled, mulatto girl—almost white even. She told me about her daily duties of helping Mrs. Washington bathe and dress as her personal maid. Her work was not hard, but she wearied of having to tend to Washington's needs. The Washingtons occasionally gave her money to go see a play, the circus, or the Tumbling Feats. She told me about her desire to find her freedom up North. She told me of her deepest desire to be free, especially as she had learned the Washingtons had promised to pass her on to their granddaughter.

Yet, she longed for better days. She longed for the freedom of home. She was not satisfied with how the Washingtons 'took care' of her. She admitted they treated her well 'They took care of all their property, the house, the land, their furniture, their pigs, their slaves. I am not a piece of property, Reverend,' she vehemently argued. She was aware of the Fugitive Slave Act that stated she could be dragged back to Mount Vernon. 'I know the law, sir, but Reverend Allen, I had to leave my mother, my family, and all that I knew. It will be a chance for me. Nothing will endanger my heart and soul more than remaining a slave. I shall know a deeper peace. A peace that I have never known.'"

Reverend Allen looked down at the pulpit for a moment. "She made me swear not to reveal her plans. That promise I have kept to this day. The last thing I heard her say was to the shoes she purchased from me, 'You belong to the Washingtons, but I do not. Tonight, you will stay here, and I will walk away as a free woman.' I can remember that feeling of deep longing. I spent many a day and night sitting creekside, pleading with God to rescue me from Master Sturgis."

"Testify!" a loud female voice rang out.

"Honestly, I wish I could have helped her cause. I can respect anyone who desires to be separated from the bondage of slavery, but if he who broke the yoke of British burdens from off the neck of the people of this land, and was hailed his country's deliverer, by what name shall we call him who secretly and almost unknown emancipated his bondmen and bondwomen—became to them a father, and gave them an inheritance. I should also mention his former cook, Chef Hercules, who I am told made the most sumptuous delicacies. Him, I never had the opportunity to meet, but wherever he is, I wish him peace," Allen declared.

"Alright, now." A woman in a colored frock waved her fan with her right hand.

"Washington was a slaver, indeed, but I do believe his heart was in the right place. He had talked about his plans to give gradual manumission to his slaves. He and I may not have agreed on the timeline, for I wanted slavery to end with undue speed, but he felt like it its time was 'not yet.'"

"Yes, now! If not now, when?" an excited parishioner called out.

"It is not often necessary, and it is seldom that occasion requires recommending the observance of the laws of the land to you, but at this time it becomes a duty; for you cannot honor those who have loved you and been your benefactors more than by taking their council and advice," Allen said as he wiped his brow of sweat.

"You may be of the ilk to celebrate this occasion. I do urge you to curb your enthusiasm. And here let me entreat you always to bear in mind the affectionate farewell advice of the great Washington— to love your country, to obey its laws, to seek its peace, and to keep yourselves from attachment to any foreign nation," Allen stated.

"I'm not hosting a barbecue at the house or anything, but I, for one, will not be crying," Brother Gray called out.

"Your observance of these short and comprehensive expressions will make you good citizens and greatly promote the cause of the oppressed and shew to the world that you hold dear the name of George Washington. I implore you," Allen stated.

"I am not that forgiving, Pastor. I say one less slaver in the world is better than honoring this man," added a man.

"I understand completely your feelings, sir." Pastor Allen softened his tone. "Yet, I forgive as Christ forgave me. May a double portion of his spirit rest on all the officers of the government in the United States, and all that say my Father, my Father—the chariots of Israel, and the horsemen thereof, which is the whole of the American people.

"You may feel no love lost for President Washington but think of his wife and his children. Think of what he did in the revolution. Deeds like these are not common. He did not let his right hand know what his left hand did, but he who sees in secret will openly reward such acts of beneficence."

Allen paused, looking at his congregants who had braved the cold to attend church that day. He saw the snow had piled into the corners of the windows. He wiped sweat from his brow that threatened to drip from his forehead even though many in the congregation had not removed their winter coats. Some cinched their coats. His eyes flashed toward the orange glow from the fire in the forge. He wondered if he had arrived early enough to get the fire going to warm the church for today's services.

"It's December of 1799 and here we sit on the eve of a new century. I would have thought American's dependence on slavery would have abated. American slavery should have been over with one verse … one verse would have changed it forever. One verse. Exodus twenty-one, verse sixteen, says anybody caught kidnapping another person and then selling them will receive capital punishment. You could be killed if you kidnap somebody and if you sell them." He pounded the desk as his speaking pace became more rapid. "American slavery was based on kidnapping and selling folk. If that one verse was taught and preached and applied, slavery would have been over because everybody was subject to death since the Old Testament was being used to promote it. But because of greed which means 'I want the profit,' 'I want the income,' 'I want the power,' 'I want the benefit,' 'I want it' … because of greed people were held hostage by kidnapping and selling while the church has acquiesced. Because when you abandon God and his word slavery rules on all levels," Allen protested.

"Yes!"

"Amen, sir!"

"You're talking good now."

Allen paused and considered what he had been saying. He surveyed the audience, and his gaze landed on the face of his wife Flora who was seated on the front pew. Allen mopped his brow one more time and then welcomed Flora to the platform. He stepped down to provide her assistance to the stage.

"Flora, why don't you come up and bless us with your voice.

Sing a hymn for us, would you? This is a weighty moment. Would you just honor us with your voice?"

Flora stood and came to the front of the church. She walked with her head lowered, her head covered with a white scarf.

"We sing the mighty power of God,
*   that made the mountains rise,*
That spread the flowing seas abroad
*   and built the lofty skies.*
We sing the wisdom that ordained
*   the sun to rule the day.*
The moon shines full at his command,
*   and all the stars obey."*

Flora welled up with tears and her voice trembled, but her words rang confident as she sang the chorus.

"We sing the goodness of the Lord,
*   who filled the earth with food;*
he formed the creatures through the word,
*   and then pronounced them good.*
Lord, how thy wonders are displayed,
*   where'er we turn our eyes,*
If we survey the ground we tread,
*   or gaze upon the sky."*

Flora repeated the final line, "or gaze upon the sky," and quietly returned to her seat.

Allen returned to the podium and concluded the service with a prayer of benediction. "Saints, truly a solemn service, but God is still on the throne and worthy of praise. To him, be the glory. Go in peace and God go with you."

Chapter 16

An Abundance of Rain
1797–1807

The saints were tremendously riled. They had been singing songs and dancing before the Lord in high praise. Sister Thomas had brought her washboard and played it with a spoon, scraping it rhythmically in time with the clapping of hands of the people.

Reverend Allen quietly approached the podium. "Shh … Do you hear what I hear?"

The parishioners quieted and looked around in a state of confusion. Each looked at the other with raised eyebrows.

Pastor Allen put his finger up to his lips and whispered, "Do you hear what I hear?"

Sister Thomas answered, "Am I supposed to be hearing something?"

"The children of Israel had been experiencing a famine. It had not rained in over three years."

"Lord, have mercy," a female voice shouted aloud.

"And Elijah had been in discussion with the prophets of Baal. It was a bit of an argument, really. They were having a 'whose God is better?' session. Elijah had just proven to the prophets of Baal whose God was better. He had stood flatfooted and built an altar and placed wood on it. He challenged his opponents to pour gallons of water on the wood. Not only once but twice and then a third time. The scriptures say that the trench around the altar had filled with water. The sacrifice and the wood had to have been soaked."

"My Lord!" a deacon shouted.

"Elijah goaded the prophets of Baal. He told them that whoever's God answered by fire was the true God. The Baal prophets called out to their God for hours. They chanted and cut themselves with knives, but their god did not answer. They had cried and begged and pleaded, Elijah poked at them suggesting that their god must be sleeping."

"Amen," a brother said.

"The four hundred and fifty prophets had called out for hours and hours. Their god was silent. Elijah, however, was confident in his faith and sure his God would answer when he said just sixty-four words in his prayer." Allen turned his Bible pages and read the prayer found in 1 Kings 18:36, 37, "'Lord God of Abraham, Isaac, and of Israel, let it be known this day that thou art God in Israel, and that I am thy servant, and that I have done all these things at thy word. Hear me, O Lord, hear me, that this people may know that thou art the Lord God, and that thou hast turned their heart back again.'"

"Amen, brother. Hear us, Father," a female voice agreed.

"Immediately, the fire of the Lord fell consuming the meat of the sacrifice, the wood, the stones even the dust, and licked up the water in the trench. This should make all of you aware that you do not need fancy words when you pray—only faith in the God you are praying to. No need to pray fancy long-winded prayers. A simple sixty-four words prayer of faith was sufficient. But hear me when I say this—your obedience to God is essential to seeing God manifest. Elijah told the Lord 'I have done all these things at thy word.' Your obedience is a must to see God's hand moving. He said, 'Obedience is better than sacrifice.'" Allen stepped down off the podium to get closer to the congregation.

"When I was just seventeen, I heard God call me. I was sitting down by the creek bank, and the Lord called me to preach his word to declare his message to the slave and to the free. I knew the despair in the waiting. 'Lord, this is Richard the Negro, I am not important enough to deliver your word.' When we would think that our day's work was never done, we often thought that after our master's death we were liable to be sold to the highest bidder. Master Sturgis was much in debt and thus my troubles were increased, and I was often brought to weep between the porch and the altar. I went to my master and sought a plan to gain my freedom. Now, it took me six years to do it, but I paid for mine and my brother's manumission. A door had finally swung open and with the Lord's help, I walked through it."

Voices rang out in praise to the Lord. "Hallelujah!"

"I had found Methodism. I was not going to be Richard the Negro anymore. I was a freed man. I attended classes where I learned to read and write. Suddenly, my dungeon shook, my chains flew off, and glory to God, I cried. My soul was filled. I cried, enough for me—the Savior died."

"Yes! Praise the Lord!" Many folks clapped their hands and waved their arms as they joined Allen as he told his story of conversion.

"I had been a slave all my life. My parents had been sold off. I never saw them again, but I believe God has a mission for me. There had been no rain for three years, but God promised rain. Slavery looked like it would never end, but God showed me there was a work for me to do. So back in the book of 1 Kings 18, Elijah went to Ahab and told him 'Get thee up, eat and drink, for there is a sound of an abundance of rain.'" Allen returned to the podium. "Ahab sent his servant to the hills seven times. He returned six times with a negative report but on the seventh time, he said 'Behold, there arises out of the sea a little cloud the size of a man's fist.'" Allen read from his Bible, "'And it came to pass in the meanwhile, that the heaven was black with clouds and wind, and there was great rain.'"

"Yes!" Praises rang out around the church. "Amen."

"Manifestation is preceded by a sound. In the second chapter of Acts, the disciples and others were gathered in an upper room for Pentecost. 'And suddenly there came a sound from heaven, as of a rushing mighty wind, and it filled the house where they were sitting.' That sound ushered in the promised Holy Spirit. Do you want to hear the sound?"

"Yes!" The congregation shouted. "Yessir!"

"Then, come up to this altar, bow your knees, and repent. That is what is called for in this day. We need to repent before the Lord for our complacency and acceptance of the sin of slavery and for our lack of obedience to the Almighty. The Bible says, 'Repent and be baptized in the name of Jesus Christ for the remission of your sins.'" Allen slapped his palm on the podium. "You may say I am not guilty of the sin of slavery. I have never owned slaves, but the Bible declares, 'For all have sinned and fall short of the glory of God.' This word is for you."

Allen prayed for those who surrounded the altar. As he concluded his prayer, he opened his eyes and spied the quorum of white men in suits who had flanked the rear of the sanctuary.

"Brethren, what do I owe for this privilege today? Why are you here?" Allen held his hand on his hip.

"We are here to challenge the appropriateness of this church. The church and its land are owned by the Methodist Church," the man stated.

"Sir, you are mistaken. This church has been purchased with our money and your challenge is wrong. We have the blessing of the Methodist conference to have this as our church," Richard Allen said. "It was even blessed by Bishop Asbury. We are a fully licensed body having ownership of this building—not the Methodist conference."

"We intend to bring you before the conference to insist you owe money to the conference for this land and this building," the man said. "This church belongs to the conference, and you need to surrender it to us. You need to give me the keys and the books of the church."

"Sir, if I may, we are just concluding our services. Leave me to finish up, and then we can meet in the office," Allen said.

Allen concluded services and joined the white gentlemen at the rear of the church. "Gentlemen, come this way please." The pastor led his guests to the makeshift office near the entrance of the church.

When everyone was seated, Allen started his complaint. "Now, I don't appreciate y'all coming into and interrupting my service like a bunch of soldiers."

"Perhaps you are bothered because we are all white? This is a black church, right?"

"Whites are welcomed here. Anyone is welcome here. African is in the name only to stipulate that Black people are the founders not the only attendees. We have white members of our congregation," Allen said. "And let me speak to your rude claims. We owe nothing to the Methodist church, and we resent the implication. We are a standalone entity."

Once he saw that Allen was recalcitrant and could not be moved, the gentleman tried another tactic. "I just want to help you. You obviously need some help to understand the legal arguments regarding possession and title of a church being incorporated. I will draw up the incorporation papers myself, and you won't have to pay a dime. Can you agree to that?"

"We obviously need legal help, and your assistance offer is appreciated. Yes, we accept," Allen said. "Your argument has fallen on listening ears."

"Fine. I'll draw up the required papers. I'll bring them by in a few days," the gentleman said, then motioned for the other white to follow him out.

Ten years later, another Methodist minister challenged Allen's ownership of the church stating it belonged to the Methodist conference. Allen reached out to a friend of his, a white lawyer, for help.

"But we have the incorporation papers," said Allen.

"You are right." His friend reached into his black case and pulled out the paperwork. "These papers have your signature giving ownership to the Methodist denomination," said the white lawyer.

Allen grew angry. "Oh, he duped us. I trusted him and he tricked us. I fell for it. I can't believe I trusted him, and he bamboozled me. Now what do I do?"

"I can help you. There is a way out of this. If you can get two-thirds of your membership to vote to alter the incorporation papers, then it can be done," the lawyer said.

Allen took all that he learned back to his congregation who unanimously voted to change the incorporation. Despite numerous attempts by the Methodist leaders, and a lengthy court case, the case was settled by the Supreme Court of Philadelphia. Bethel belonged to the Africans not the Methodist Church. The church made a resplendent sound the next Sunday.

Chapter 17

THE LAST GOODBYE
1801

Honey, I'm weary of being in this bed. Will you take me on a walk?" Flora asked her husband.

"Certainly. Do you think you're up to a walk?" Richard asked with concern.

"I just can't take staying in this bed anymore. I'm going stir crazy. I have counted every dot in this ceiling over and over," Flora admitted with disgust.

"Yes, I'll take you for a walk if you want," Richard said. "Let's get you dressed."

Richard helped his wife put on a few layers of clothes.

"Richard, why are you putting so many clothes on me?" she protested.

"It is cold outside. I simply want you to be warm and bundled up."

"You worry too much. I don't need you to be worried about me," said Flora, shrugging off another scarf.

"It's my job to worry. You are my wife and I'm supposed to be taking care of you," said Richard.

"I know, but you do too much. I've become a burden. You cook for me, help me get dressed, and help me take a bath. I've become a nuisance, I'm afraid," Flora said, trying to bolster herself to appear stronger as she balanced herself against the bed and tried to avoid her husband's gaze.

Richard bent over to tie his and her shoes. "Alright. Let's go. I'll get your coat."

As he helped her down the front steps of their home, Flora cinched her coat tighter. "Brr, it is brisk out here. Deceptively chilly, despite the sun. I really appreciate you taking me out, Richard. I just couldn't look at the same walls anymore." Tears welled up in her eyes.

"What's wrong, my dear? Why are you crying?" Richard reached out to comfort his ailing wife.

She had been sick for many months now, and Richard had exhausted every avenue of healing.

"Oh, nothing," said Flora wiping her eyes, "I've just been thinking about how much you have sacrificed. I wish we had children, so someone could share your burden."

Richard choked back tears too, but he wanted to only give her good thoughts. "We've reached the river. There's the very spot I was in where I felt I heard the Lord call me to preach, and I said, 'yes' to him."

"This spot?"

"Yes. This spot." He pointed. "I had been called to preach his word, and I promised God to follow his direction to accomplish his will."

Flora sighed with a heavy breath, then turned her face to the late winter sun. "It sure is beautiful out here today."

"Sure is," said Richard.

They walked farther along the bank of the river until Flora pointed to a patch of green sprouts along the edge.

"Look! New life springing forth."

"Spring does approach," Richard agreed.

He was glad of the green today. It had been a long, cold winter. But March had begun, and with it, the promise of renewal.

"Richard, I've been meaning to talk to you about something."

Allen turned to his wife and took her hands in his own. "Yes, dear. Tell me. Here, let me help you sit down." Richard took Flora by the arm and helped her sit on a stump. "What is it?"

"Richard, I've been thinking about who will help you carry on when I'm gone." Flora's voice tone changed. "When I've gone the last mile of the way."

"Flora, don't talk so. I don't want to think about such things."

"Do you know who I believe would be a great partner for you? Someone who could serve with you in ministry and help carry the load for you?" Flora asked. "Sarah Bass. I think she'd be a good wife for you and could possibly give you children. She has those child-bearing hips, you know." Flora's lips trembled.

"Oh, my dear, that is not something I worry about. The Lord has given me so many children to care for. They may not be mine, but they're mine."

Flora put her hand against her husband's cheek. "Richard, that is why I love you so much. You are so concerned about others. That's why I thought about Sarah. You deserve someone to look after you."

"I'm just not worried about finding another wife. You are my wife and that is enough," Richard said, pulling her hand to his mouth for a kiss.

"Husband, you are so obstinate. Maybe the Lord is trying to tell you something," Flora said.

"The Lord be praised. Let his will be done. I will follow his lead just like I did when I got that old, blind horse for free after Master Sturgis allowed me to purchase my freedom," Richard said with a smile.

"That is a good attitude to have, my love." Flora brushed a fallen leaf from his shoulder. "Now help me up. I want to go see what is growing over there."

"Are you sure you're up to that?"

"Yes, it's what I must do," Flora said.

Richard watched as his frail wife stepped gingerly around the river's edge. The Lord was pleased to strengthen us, and remove all fear from us, and disposed our hearts to be as useful as possible. When he noticed Flora had reached the intended spot, he sat down on the bank. He soon drifted off to sleep but startled awake sometime later. Flora was not to be found. He frantically searched and found her body beneath the river. A large stone sat on her chest.

He cried and moaned aloud as he mourned the loss of his wife for several moments. Then he ran to Absalom's nearby home.

He knocked frantically on their front door.

"Absalom, come quickly. I need your help. Flora has died down by the river," Richard cried.

They quickly hooked the horse to a wagon and sped away toward the river.

When they arrived at the spot, the two men jumped quickly from the wagon both arriving at the floating body in the river.

"You didn't take her out of the water?" Absalom asked with a frown.

"No, I ran to get you. I was scared and I panicked," Richard admitted. "Help me get her out of there, please."

The duo worked together to pull Flora from the river.

A few days later, Flora's body lay at the front of the church. Richard cried and wept aloud. Absalom had been invited to officiate the funeral, but he had asked Richard to give final remarks.

"Alas, my Flora is gone. I'm sad for multiple reasons, but I'm most sad I did not get to say … goodbye."

Chapter 18

Wedding Bells
1802

Richard, do you take this woman to be your married wife—to live together in the bonds of holy matrimony? Will you promise to honor and cherish her if you both shall live?"

"Yes, sir, I will," Allen promptly agreed while smiling.

"And Miss Sarah, I will ask you the same. Will you promise to honor and cherish Richard if you both shall live?"

"I will." Sarah smiled as she answered.

The preacher, balanced on his heels behind the rostrum, nodded. "Marriage is one expression of the many varieties of love. Love is one, though its expressions are infinite. It is fitting to speak briefly about love. We live in a world of joy and fear and search for meaning and strength in seeming disorder. We discover the truest guidelines to our quest when we realize love in all its magnitudes. Love is the eternal force of life. Love is the force that allows us to face fear and uncertainty with courage."

He continued, "As Jesus' first miracle was at the wedding in Cana of Galilee, I charge you today to keep Christ at the center of your marriage covenant. If you would have the foundation of your union be the love you have for each other, not just at this moment, but for all the days ahead, then cherish the hopes and dreams that you bring here today."

Reading from the notes he held in his hands, he instructed, "Resolve that your love will never be blotted out by the commonplace nor obscured by the ordinary in life. Devotion, joy, and love can grow only if you nurture them together. Stand fast in that hope and confidence, believing in your shared future just as strongly as you believe in yourselves and in each other today. In this spirit, you can create a partnership that will strengthen and sustain you all the days of your lives."

The minister continued, "Richard, as you stare into the glimmering eyes of Sarah, your love, I want you to know that she will not always be this beautiful. There will be days when the smile is not as radiant as it is today." The crowd giggled. "Sarah, there will be days when Richard is not the reason for your happy smile. What am I saying? I am promising that life is not full of sunshine and rainbows but of pain and sadness. Richard, I am sure you recall how sickness stole your first wife, Flora, away from you."

Richard teared up and wiped his eyes with his handkerchief. He caught the eyes of his friend, Absalom, standing in the line beside him. Absalom had stood by him through his grief and now stood with him in his happiness.

"And there will be days where you may both not even like each other, but I charge you to remember what you feel today in those times."

Richard squeezed Sarah's hands in his own as she giggled.

The minister addressed the audience next. "Who gives this woman to this man?"

"Her mother and I do," Sarah's father answered.

"Excellent." The minister smiled. "Sarah, will you have this man to be your husband, to live together in the covenant of marriage? Will you love him, comfort him, honor and keep him, in sickness and in health, and forsaking all others, be faithful to him if you both shall live? Signify by saying 'I will.'"

When Sarah had agreed in the affirmative, the pastor turned to Richard, "Richard, will you have this woman to be your wife, to live together in the covenant of marriage? Will you love her, comfort her, honor and keep her, in sickness and in health, and forsaking all others, be faithful to her if you both shall live? Signify by saying 'I will.'"

Richard agreed and then the minister turned to the gathered audience. "Will all of you witnessing these promises do all in your power to uphold these two persons in their marriage? Signify by saying 'I will.'"

The audience agreed.

"Richard, please repeat after me. I, Richard, take you, Sarah, to be my wedded wife, to have and to hold from this day forward, for better for worse, for richer for poorer, in sickness and in health, to love and to cherish till death do us part, according to God's holy ordinance; and thereto I plight thee my troth."

Richard repeated the words as instructed.

"Richard, I ask you today, will you stand by Sarah, care for her, hold her in the highest regard and die with this love you have for her untarnished in your heart? Please answer 'I will.'"

"Sarah, please repeat after me. I, Sarah take you, Richard, to be my wedded husband, to have and to hold from this day forward, for better, for worse, for richer, for poorer, in sickness and in health, to love and to cherish till death do us part, according to God's holy ordinance; and thereto I give thee my troth."

Sarah repeated her vows as instructed.

The couple stood facing each other and smiled. Then Richard began his own vows.

"I take you, Sarah, to be my wife and I promise before God and all who are present here to be your loving and faithful husband, if our lives shall last. I will serve you with tenderness and respect and encourage you to develop God's gifts in you. Today, I give myself to you in marriage. I promise to encourage and inspire you, to laugh with you, and to comfort you in times of sorrow and struggle. I promise to love you in good times and in bad, when life seems easy and when it seems hard, when our love is simple, and when it is an effort. I promise to cherish you, and to always hold you in highest regard. These things I give to you today, and all the days of our life."

Sarah smiled, then repeated his vows as her own. "I take you, Richard, to be my husband; and I promise before God and these witnesses to be your loving and faithful wife; in plenty and in want; in joy and in sorrow; in sickness and in health if we both shall live. Today I give myself to you in marriage. I promise to encourage and inspire you, to laugh with you, and to comfort you in times of sorrow and struggle. I promise to love you in good times and in bad, when life seems easy and when it seems hard, when our love is simple, and when it is an effort. I promise to cherish you, and to always hold you in highest regard. These things I give to you today, and all the days of our life."

"Sarah, the wife of a pastor will face difficult days," the minister continued. "At times, the church will take priority over you. Will you stand by Richard, care for him, hold him in the highest regard and die with this love you have for him untarnished in your heart? Please answer 'I will,'"

Sarah answered, "I definitely will."

The minister paused as he gave his final declarations. "This is a moment of celebration. Let it also be a moment of dedication. The world does a good job of reminding us of how fragile we are. Individuals are fragile; relationships are fragile too. Every marriage needs the love, nurture, and support of a network of friends and family. And now, by the power vested in me as a preacher of the gospel, I now pronounce you husband and wife. Let us pray."

The minister bowed his head with Richard and Sarah.

"Heavenly Father, may your strength and glory overshadow this couple as they endeavor to do your will. May your peace be in their home, and should your will include adding children to their fold, may those children live to serve you and bring their parents' honor. In Jesus's name, amen."

The audience clapped. Several people hooted.

The minister announced, "I now present to you all for the first time, the Reverend Richard and Mrs. Sarah Allen. What God has joined together, let no man put asunder. Richard, go ahead and kiss your bride."

The Allens kissed and smiled as they embraced each other and looked out at their family and friends who celebrated with them.

"On this wedding day," the minister concluded, "I charge you as friends and family to not only to be friends of Richard or Sarah but friends of Richard and Sarah together, friends of the relationship. May the love you have found grow in meaning and strength until its beauty is shown in a common devotion to all that is compassionate and life-giving. May the flow of your love help brighten the face of the earth. May the source of all love touch and bless us and grace our lives with color and courage."

Richard and Sarah Allen had six children. Sarah Allen was highly active in what became the AME Church and is called the "Founding Mother." As Mrs. Allen, Sarah would prove to be of great service to Bethel and Pastor Allen. She fit the model of a good republican woman responsible for bringing dignity and moral culture to their home. Sarah ensured the Allen home was never shut up to the needs of the poor and penniless.

Chapter 19

A WOMAN PREACHER?
1811–19

Ah, yes, Pastor, do come in." Jarena Lee welcomed Pastor Allen into her home.

Allen removed his overcoat. "Thank you, Jarena. And where is Joseph?"

Jarena moved to hang the coat up in the foyer. "Oh, he will be right down. We have been wanting to sit with you for dinner for quite some time." Jarena smiled.

"It smells just wonderful. Do I smell field beans?"

"My, you have a good nose. Yes, I made you some field peas. Sister Sarah mentioned how much you liked them at a recent women's league meeting. So I thought I would fix you some. Got some collard greens that been cooking all day too," Jarena said with another smile.

Just then, Joseph bounded down the stairs and jumped off the next to last step. "Ooh, we fixing to eat good! I hope you brought your appetite, Pastor."

Rubbing his hands together, Allen gushed, "I'm a black preacher. I always bring my appetite."

"Then let's eat. I am sure the pastor's schedule is busy, so we shouldn't tarry," Jarena said, directing traffic to the table.

"I hope you didn't go through too much trouble," Pastor Allen confided.

"No trouble at all. Come on, y'all men sit down at the table, and I'll get the meal served up." Jarena exited the dining area.

"Ugh," Joseph said, grunting as he sat in his chair.

"Tough day, Joseph?" Richard said.

"Not terrible, Pastor. It's just these old, weary bones, I guess," Joseph said. "God's been too good to me to complain."

Jarena entered the room carrying a plate of rolls in one hand and a plate of sliced tomatoes in the other. She placed the tomatoes right next to Pastor Allen. His eyes relished the sight.

"My goodness, don't that look good. I ain't had beans and tomatoes in a month of Sundays." Allen stirred the beans in the bowl they had been served in.

"Here, Pastor, you want some rice? Field beans and rice go together right," Joseph said with pride. He scooped from the serving bowl before Allen could answer.

"Oh, yessir. I'll have some," Allen said as he lifted his plate to receive the bounty offered.

The trio ate as they served each other. When they had fared sumptuously, Jarena's convivial attitude turned to business.

"Pastor, I have asked you here because I want to talk to you about something serious."

"Yes, Sister Lee. Ask away," Allen said.

Jarena turned her head toward her husband and sighed deeply. "Well, Pastor, I believe the Lord has called me to preach."

Allen coughed as he drank water from a glass. "Preach? You? Your husband is a preacher. You've seen what he has had to experience each week. Why would you want to bring that on yourself?"

"It's not what I want. It's what I am called to do," Jarena pushed back.

"The Methodist Church does not make provision for women preachers," Allen said.

"But if a man may preach, because the Savior died for him, why not the woman, seeing he died for her also? Is he not a whole Savior, instead of half of one?" Jarena expressed her own objection.

Allen did not have a comeback and looked to Joseph for help. Perhaps objections from her husband would satisfy Jarena.

"Don't look at me. I've already told her my objections," said Joseph. "She assures me there will be no affect upon her duties here at home."

"Now, before you start the argument that 'women should keep silent in the church,' I will ask you, did not Mary first preach the risen Savior? Oh, how careful ought we to be lest through our bylaws of church government and discipline we bring into disrepute even the word of life for as unseemly as it may appear nowadays for a woman to preach, it should be remembered that 'nothing is impossible with God,' and why should it be thought impossible, heterodox, or improper for a woman to preach seeing the Savior died for the woman as well as the man. Is not the resurrection of Jesus the climax of Christianity? Mary preached the gospel of the resurrection." Jarena wiped her face with a napkin and drank a sip of water.

She restarted her argument. "Some would argue that there have been no women talking because women are uneducated. If having an education was necessary, most of the disciples would have been disallowed from ministry. You may wish to argue 1 Timothy, chapter two, but I come back with are only husbands to lift holy hands in prayer without anger and disputing? Are only *wives* to dress modestly, have good deeds, and worship God," Jarena said, raising her voice. "If God is no 'respecter of persons,' why would he put this calling in my heart? I suspect if he wants someone to do something in his name, then he or she should be allowed to do it without prohibition."

"See. She's ready," said Joseph.

"I am not settled on it yet," said Allen. "I am not able to commend women to be pastors but as teachers of the word of God. The only activity women are restricted from is teaching or having spiritual authority over men. This bars women from serving as pastors to men."

"I don't want to be a pastor," argued Jarena. "Simply a servant. I don't want to have authority over men, but only to help them understand the message of God. This does not make women less important, by any means. Rather, it gives them a ministry focus more in agreement with God's design. Women excel in the gifts of hospitality, mercy, teaching, and evangelism—all things necessary in the local church. Imagine if there were no women in the church. I am only committed to speaking a simple message of the birth, life, death, and resurrection of our Lord, and accompany it with power to the sinner's heart. As for me, I am fully persuaded that the Lord called me to labor according to what I have received in his vineyard. If he has not, how could he consistently bear testimony in favor of my poor labors in awakening and converting sinners."

"You have given me much to think about, Sister Lee, and a full belly." Allen rose from the table and made for the door. "Let me continue to think on it and I will get back with you."

1818

On a rare occasion, Rev. Allen got to spend the afternoon with his wife at home. One such afternoon, his wife asked, "Dear, do you know Jarena Lee? She's been attending the church for a while. She has two children and is a widow—her husband died a few months back."

"Yes, I know Sister Lee," Allen responded, "she wants to preach."

"Oh, so you know." Sarah raised her eyebrows. "And why have you not given her the opportunity? She will probably be a great help to you. You wouldn't have to preach so much."

"Sarah, you know that would go against the policies of the Methodist Church. The elders would be none too pleased." Richard shook his head and laughed.

"I can recall not too long ago you were willing to stand against the Methodists when they were against your idea of an all-black

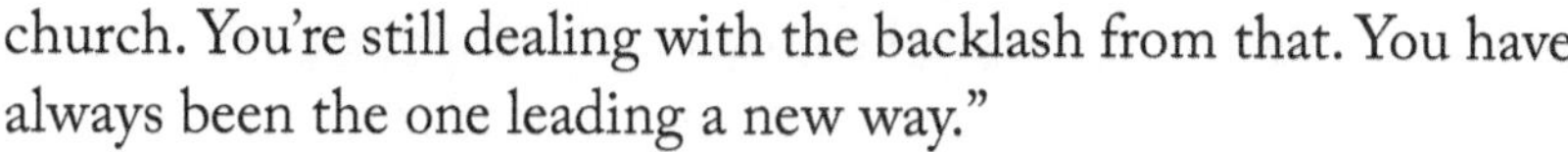

church. You're still dealing with the backlash from that. You have always been the one leading a new way."

Richard cocked an eyebrow her way.

"Well," she continued, "Jarena is coming over for tea."

Allen sighed. "I imagine you are right. She has been persistent in her requests for the last few years. I just don't think now is the time to ruffle any more feathers over this issue."

"You don't want to ruffle feathers. Who are you? The Reverend Richard Allen I knew, and thought I married, believes in ruffling feathers when something is wrong."

"Is it wrong?" Allen asked.

Sarah sat beside him at the table and pointed a finger at him. "Well, my Bible reads in Joel 2:28 that 'in the last days, your sons and daughters will prophesy.' And daughters." She raised her eyebrows again at him. "I don't understand your reticence."

"And the Apostle Paul followed that up with 'Let your women keep silence in the churches: for it is not permitted unto them to speak; but they are commanded to be under obedience as also saith the law,'" Allen retorted. "It's just not the custom to allow women to preach. Can you name one church anywhere where a woman is the preacher? Just name one," Allen dared his wife.

"Can you name one church where the pastor and congregation are all black?" she shot back. "I can. Bethel. And that's because you stood up to the Church and pushed against convention," she said.

When Richard gave no further argument, she added, "She should be here in a few minutes. Promise me, you will hear her out."

"Yes, wife," Allen cajoled.

A few minutes later, Jarena knocked on the door. Mrs. Allen welcomed the woman into the living room where Pastor Allen sat. Jarena directed her children to "Go out back and play." They followed the instruction of their mother.

"Jarena, I know why you're here," Allen began. "It's just improbable going against Methodist discipline which knows little of women preachers."

Jarena sat in the chair he indicated and removed her gloves. "That may be true, but are you not the leader of the African Methodists?"

Before he could reply, a crash came from where the children had been playing. Standing, she yelled, "What are you all doing? I don't know what I am going to do with them kids."

Allen jumped on this opportunity. "And that is my point, Jarena, wouldn't your children be better served by a mother who is not also a preacher?"

Jarena sat back down and smoothed out her skirts before speaking, "Pastor, have you ever wanted to do more … to be more … more than what your circumstances dictate? From the time I began serving God, I have felt something in my craw, 'Preach the gospel. Go preach the gospel. I will put words in your mouth.' I put my life on hold, but ever since my husband died, the call has come back. Since when my parents sent me at seven years old to be a live-in maid with that white family, I have known there was something more for me than being a wife and mother."

Her fervent persistence gave Allen pause. "Let me think and pray on it, Jarena. I will get back to you soon."

1819

Today, Allen and his congregation would be fed by another preacher who was the invited guest. He proudly watched as the parishioners praised and shouted and danced before the Lord. He smiled and tapped his foot to the rhythm of the drumming. When it was time, he invited the guest to the podium to preach. The man's text was from the book of Jonah. Allen watched as the man began, but suddenly, fell gripped by silence.

Jarena Lee jumped to the guest preacher's aid. She stood nervously in the pulpit, her voice quivering but confident. She directed the crowd to attend to the first chapter of Jonah.

Jarena preached, "I was like Jonah. I was a wretched sinner. I wanted to ignore God's calling and run away to the farthest part of the world, but God called me. He wanted me to preach repentance to the sinner. And I was not about to get thrown overboard into the sea and swallowed by a great fish for disobedience. I would say what had to be said. I would not let the traditions of man hinder me from doing what God had for me to do. I said, 'not me Lord.' I likened myself to Moses in that when I stood before the burning bush, I reminded God I'm not adequate for task—I don't know enough, people won't take me seriously, I'm no good with words, I'm not willing. I stand before you today a woman who has been delivered, set free from the expectations of people, who is ready to proclaim the gospel of Jesus Christ."

"When I was younger," she said. "I held onto malice in my heart, but I let it go by asking forgiveness from God. When I did that, the malice was gone, and the glory of the Lord washed over me. It changed me."

As she prayed for the congregation and concluded the service, Allen sat astonished at how she had commanded the congregation and her knowledge of the scriptures.

Jarena sat down again with wide eyes. Perhaps wondering if she would be expelled from the church.

Allen rose in the assembly and related that she had called upon him many years before to be permitted to preach.

"After this sermon today, I believe Mrs. Lee is called to the work as any of the preachers present," he told those assembled. "I feel like I need to speak on the propriety of this woman here as a minister of the gospel. Some of you all have a problem with her and with me because I permitted her today. This holy woman living a godly life has entered this pulpit with my sanction. David wore the priestly ephod because when you are saved and sanctified and filled with the Holy Ghost, the Lord calls you king or queen or priest. If George Washington, a known slaver, wanted to speak here, none of you would have a problem, so I allow this woman to share the gospel. I have no objections. Preach on, Minister Lee. Do the work of the Lord. Save the lost. Set the captive free. Let him use you."

Chapter 20

Meeting with Asbury
1815

Bishop, it's so good to see you. It has been too long," Allen extended his hand as Asbury dismounted from his horse. Allen hoped his wide grin demonstrated how he had missed the elder preacher.

"Yes, it has, Brother Allen," Asbury returned the brotherly affection. "How are things with your health? I had heard you had fought with that horrible yellow fever contagion."

"Yes, I did. A nasty disease, but I am doing well. I had headaches, chills, an upset stomach, and a nagging pain in my chest. All this in addition to raging fevers and yellowish complexion. I was in the hospital from September to well into November. I was not out of the woods for long that I was called into service for the many who had been afflicted. Good, better, best. Never let it rest until your good is better and your better is best," said Allen.

"I imagine so. How have you fared since the war? 1812 and 1813 saw its own fair share of tensions as Britain sought to take America back," Asbury said.

"Yes. I am sure it counted its losses as they considered life since the Revolution." Allen gestured for Asbury to sit down on the bucket he had turned upside down. "Here, please sit."

"Oh, I am fine standing." Asbury waved him off. "I've been

on the back of that horse for many miles now." He smiled, then patted the neck of his horse. "Tell me, how are things with the church? I'm to understand the white people had been giving you all trouble about who rightfully owns your space."

"Yes, they were stalwart—almost to the point where they tried to persuade the members of my congregation to leave and return to St. George's, despite their threats to disown us. The congregation, thankfully, had not forgotten how St. George's had mistreated us, and their appeal went nowhere." Allen spit to his left. "They took us to court, but their petition was empty, and the courts decided in our favor."

"It's almost like Britain and the United States, isn't it? America fought the great Revolution for liberty and freedom. They just do not get it. Why would the church members go back to the place where they had been denied basic human dignity?" Asbury asked.

"I said that to my congregation. I took them to the scripture in Galatians that declares 'Stand fast therefore in the liberty wherewith Christ hath made us free and be not entangled again with the yoke of bondage,'" Allen said.

"I bet that resonated." Asbury walked over to his saddlebag and grabbed a handful of hay and began to feed it to his horse. "That's good, isn't it boy?" He slapped the horse's back thigh then lifted the horse's front leg and inspected his hoof. "We need to get you some new shoes, buddy."

"I know a place you can go to. If you don't mind walking, I can show you where," Allen said. "It's not far from here."

"Oh, yes. Could we? I have been meaning to do it for a while now." He slapped the horse's haunches twice. "What do you say, boy? Let's go get you some new shoes."

The duo walked slowly toward the barn.

"I've got a good idea. Why don't you preach at my church this Sunday?" asked Allen.

"Are you sure?" Asbury's eyes widened. "But I'm white. I can't speak—or shouldn't—speak at the African church."

"I know you're white. It's not a secret." Allen smiled. "Besides, the congregation needs to see a white person sharing God's love."

"I would be honored," Asbury said, extending his hand to Allen.

The following Sunday, the congregation waved their hands in the air in praise to God as the July sun gleamed through the windows. Asbury sat in the pew next to Allen.

"We are honored today to receive Bishop Francis Asbury. Please welcome him."

The congregation clapped as Asbury approached the rostrum.

"Thank you, Reverend Allen. I am grateful for the friendship of Pastor Allen down through these last ten years. I have enjoyed the service thus far and hope I might add something meaningful from God's word." He looked out over the congregation. "I appreciate how our colored brethren are governed by the doctrine and discipline of the Methodists."

"Amen," a female voice rung out.

"Let me begin by drawing your attention to three scriptures that will form the basis of this message today. The first is from Galatians two, verses one through five, this is the Apostle Paul writing. 'Then fourteen years after I went up again to Jerusalem with Barnabas and took Titus with me also. And I went up by revelation and communicated unto them that gospel which I preach among the Gentiles, but privately to them which were of reputation, lest by any means I should run, or had run, in vain. But neither Titus, who was with me, being a Greek, was compelled to be circumcised: And that because of false brethren unawares brought in, who came in privily to spy out our liberty which we have in Christ Jesus, that they might bring us into bondage: To whom we gave place by subjection, no, not for an hour; that the truth of the gospel might continue with you.'

"If you haven't figured it out yet, I want to express the difference between liberty and freedom. They are similar, yet very different. Let us look now at Luke's gospel, chapter four, verse eighteen. This is Jesus announcing his purpose by reading from the prophet Isaiah. 'The Spirit of the Lord is upon me, because he hath anointed me to preach the gospel to the poor; he hath sent me to heal the brokenhearted, to preach deliverance to the captives, and recovering of sight to the blind, to set at liberty them that are bruised.'"

"Amen! Thank Jesus," a lone voice agreed.

"And just as Christ announced his separation from the world, we should each be similar in that profession of faith. Being a separated person means being a person with God, for God, and near God." Asbury emphasized his points with his fingers. "You've got to live in faith and obedience for his glory and manifestation of his Son."

"Amen, Bishop," a man near the front of the church agreed.

Asbury continued, "The purpose of separation is that we as God's children might persevere in salvation and holiness and to live wholly for God as our Lord and Father to convince the unbelieving world of the truth and blessing of the gospel. Let me draw your attention to Galatians five, verses one through nine. 'Stand fast therefore in the liberty wherewith Christ hath made us free and be not entangled again with the yoke of bondage. Behold, I Paul say unto you, that if ye be circumcised, Christ shall profit you nothing. For I testify again to every man that is circumcised, that he is a debtor to do the whole law. Christ is become of no effect unto you, whosoever of you are justified by the law; ye are fallen from grace. For we through the Spirit wait for the hope of righteousness by faith. For in Jesus Christ neither circumcision availeth anything, nor uncircumcision; but faith which worketh by love. Ye did run well; who did hinder you that ye should not obey the truth? This persuasion cometh not of him that calleth you. A little leaven leaveneth the whole lump.'

"Now I don't have to explain to any of you the difference between liberty and freedom. This country was supposedly founded upon the premise of liberty while scores of colored folks labored in chains while they complained against the British empire. I want to go on record by saying there are many things that are painful to me, but cannot yet be removed, especially slave-keeping and its attendant circumstances. The Lord will certainly hear the cries of the oppressed, naked, starving creatures. O, my God! Think on this land. Amen."

The congregation cried aloud, "Amen!" Several stood—including Allen—cheering their agreement.

"I implored President Washington to dismantle slavery, but he would not be moved," Asbury continued. "I spoke to some select friends about slave-keeping, but they could not bear it. This I know, God will plead the cause of the oppressed, though it gives offence to say so here, some people were persuaded, some were not, but I kept talking about it. I described the difference between liberty and freedom. I said liberty is unlimited freedom. Under liberty you can only do as much as you have been approved to do. Freedom is freedom no questions asked," Bishop Asbury said, pounding on the rostrum as he made his point.

"In Christ, you have been set free from the law of Moses. The Apostle Paul wrote in the book of Romans, chapter seven, verses four through six 'Wherefore, my brethren, ye also are become dead to the law by the body of Christ; that ye should be married to another, even to him who is raised from the dead, that we should bring forth fruit unto God. For when we were in the flesh, the motions of sins, which were by the law, did work in our members to bring forth fruit unto death. But now we are delivered from the law, that being dead wherein we were held; that we should serve in newness of spirit, and not in the oldness of the letter.'

"He that is in Christ is free! The scriptures declare it so. In my closing, I urge you to live in victory as having the freedom we received from Christ. I leave you with this final thought from Galatians two verse sixteen."

Asbury turned to the pages in his Bible. "'Knowing that a man is not justified by the works of the law, but by the faith of Jesus Christ, even we have believed in Jesus Christ, that we might be justified by the faith of Christ, and not by the works of the law: for by the works of the law shall no flesh be justified.'"

He looked up at the assembled black faces.

"Let's pray. Dear Lord, our Father in Heaven, we lift you high. We ask you to lead us into all truth. More than that, we want to ever be found doing your will. Help us to lead lives that honor you above all. And all of God's people said amen."

"Amen!" cried members of the congregation.

Allen returned to the podium and hugged Asbury. "Good word, sir."

The congregation repeated after Allen who stood with his hands raised. "May the Lord watch between me and thee, while we are absent, one from the other. This we ask in Jesus's name, amen."

Chapter 21

An Important Appointment
1816

The songs of praise had filled the house. Pastor Allen stood from the first pew and walked to the stage.

"Today, we are ever so blessed to count Bishop Asbury among our numbers today. Let's all prepare our hearts to receive a word from the Lord. Let's receive him with a hearty 'Amen.'" Allen extended his right arm out to receive Asbury who was also seated on the first pew near Sarah. He rose to his feet and adjusted his cleric's robe before he spoke.

"Thank you, Pastor Allen. I'm glad to be back with you all today. I do enjoy my time here with Bethel. I must admit, however, my assignment today is not your typical one." He turned to Pastor Allen.

"Let me say a few words about Pastor Richard Allen. He has been a friend to me lo these many years. I have served with him and he with me. He is an articulate speaker, no doubt a skill he perfected as he walked the dusty roads of Philadelphia as a young man going house to house inviting his neighbors to come to the church house."

"Amens" were shouted throughout the sanctuary.

"A former slave, Allen has no qualms with sharing how the Lord delivered him from bondage. He believes, and I have seen it demonstrated, that loving one another is an integral part of Christian service."

Richard bowed his head as Asbury talked about him.

"He has been a model of that Christian piety and has followed Jesus's teaching to 'preach liberty to those who have been oppressed' as it instructs in Luke four, verse eighteen."

"Yes, that's right, Bishop," Allen cheered.

"And I, along with the other brothers in the Methodist conference, are in agreement that we should welcome Pastor Richard Allen to the bishopric."

"Oh, my goodness!" Sarah smiled and joined the other congregants in applause.

"Today, you will be elevated to the title and position of Bishop. I don't have to tell you what a large step this is, but I believe, it is about time."

"Amen. Thank you, Bishop Asbury," said Allen, a slight smile on his face.

"You have led this congregation well ever since that horrible day when you marched out of St. George's. And I don't blame you. How many of you were a part of the exodus?"

About fifty hands went up all around the room.

"The fact that you are still here, still worshiping God is a testament to the fine leadership of Brother Allen. I don't think I would have lasted. That was nothing short of mistreatment and was not holy or Christ-like. I cannot find the words to excuse that behavior. I am glad Brother Allen walked through it with you. Together, you have started this great work here at Bethel. Looking out across this auditorium and seeing the lighter skin color of my white brothers and sisters is further evidence of the commitment to love and forgiveness that Brother Allen has shown," Asbury said.

A chorus of individuals spoke out.

"Yes."

"Amen."

"Such good people he is."

"Ever a stalwart of black uplift, he founded the Society of Free People of Color for Promoting the Instruction and School Education of Children of African Descent. He also operated night school classes, which emphasizes self-help in his students. He has not forgotten his beginnings, and he continues to lead others away from the oppression he grew up with," Asbury said. "And if I am hearing correctly, he and his wife have opened their home to the newly freed."

Several members of the congregation answered in the affirmative while trying to stay hidden among the crowd. "Now, I will have you know, this appointment does not give you permission to stop or slow up. In fact, in many ways, you now have more to do. The term bishop means overseer, and you will continue to oversee the development of our African Methodist Episcopal work. The Bible gives instruction in Paul's letter to Timothy, chapter 3, verses one through seven." Asbury turned his Bible pages to First Timothy and read verses one to seven from chapter three.

"'This is a true saying, if a man desire the office of a bishop, he desireth a good work. A bishop then must be blameless, the husband of one wife, vigilant, sober, of good behavior, given to hospitality, apt to teach; Not given to wine, no striker, not greedy of filthy lucre; but patient, not a brawler, not covetous; One that ruleth well his own house, having his children in subjection with all gravity; (For if a man know not how to rule his own house, how shall he take care of the church of God?) Not a novice, lest being lifted with pride he fall into the condemnation of the devil. Moreover, he must have a good report of them which are without; lest he fall into reproach and the snare of the devil.'

"This scripture outlines the necessary requirements of a bishop. The first indicates you must not be pursuing the office. My visit is a surprise to you, isn't it?" Asbury addressed Allen.

"Yes, sir. It is," confirmed Allen.

"And the next indicates you must be above reproach. I don't

believe anyone here would say you are not worthy of the title. Am I right?"

"No, sir," Brother Gray said from the front row.

"And he is the husband of only one wife. His partner, Sarah, sitting right there next to him in that white dress. Brother Allen gets the title, but this is her appointment too. She will be charged with carrying on the growth of the church by growing its community and its sharing attitude."

"Yes, I will," Sarah said.

"He lost his beloved Flora a while back, and I believe he and Sarah make a formidable ministry partnership," said Asbury.

"You are talking right, sir. They are the salt of the earth," Brother Gray said.

"He must not be given to strong drink or be a violent man and he must be temperate exhibiting self-control. I know men who are one way in church, but something completely different at home. I get the sense this is not Reverend Allen."

"Right," Sarah called out.

"And he must be hospitable. I believe that is Sister Sarah's doing, but I'm sure he gets it from her," said Asbury with a smile.

"I'm sure that is right." Allen turned to face Sarah and smiled.

"I say all that about Sarah, but he must be a good steward of his home and finances. Brother Allen rose from virtually nothing, but he is now one of the most financially stable black men in this county. He owns multiple properties and has been an entrepreneur owning a nail factory and maintains a shoe store in his home."

"Thank you, Jesus," Richard said.

"I don't think it needs to be said, but he must be committed to the Lord and doing his work. For this cause, Allen deserves the office and title of bishop," announced Asbury. "Can I get a witness?"

A chorus of amens rang out over the sanctuary.

"I'm of a mind to remind you of his giving heart. Years ago, he noticed my horse was aging and giving out. He bought me a new horse so I could keep doing God's work. I asked him to help me save souls by coming out on the road with me. He turned me down, opting to serve the black community. He is a man given to much prayer, as a daily ritual, not as a weekly obligation but a way of living. I'm reminded of the time in 1773 when Allen ministered the word and a negro man trembled and surrendered. The very house shook," Asbury said. "He is committed to delivering the truth in the word causing people to chase after God. He is a born revivalist. He has a message for the world. Methodists must liberate their slaves lest they be denied the Lord's Supper and expelled from the church."

Richard and Sarah stood and clapped their hands.

"Brother Allen, while you are standing. Take the hand of your wife and join me up here, please," Asbury said.

Richard followed the instructions and he and Sarah joined Asbury onstage.

"Let's receive our honoree right now with a round of applause."

The crowd responded in kind.

"Pastor Allen, I want you to remember a few things as you take this next step in ministry. I charge you with these five things. First, stay close to the Scriptures. They have been written for our transformation, and you have been called to help this community live into them. It is your responsibility to teach the Scriptures and draw people into its meanings, its prophecies, its comfort, and discomfort." Asbury held up his Bible. "The study of scripture is the chief way of finding our duty. There should be no dumb reading of the scriptures, meaning no scripture should go untranslated, unexamined, or unrevealed. Because the scriptures are about our transformation, when you bring people into them and do this faithfully, expect changes all the way around. This is what the apostle meant when we were to 'study to show ourselves a workman unto God, which is our reasonable service.'"

"Amen," a loud male voice said from the rear of the church.

Asbury turned his attention back to the Allens. "Second, nurture yourself spiritually and relationally. Pray, study, and perform your devotions with an open heart so that you can continue to grow in the sight of God. You cannot ask people to grow and change if you are not doing the same. When you do this, expect changes."

"Yes, sir," Richard said.

Asbury continued, "Third, remember, although you are the bishop, God has made us all spiritually equal. You are no better or worse than any who gather here seeing your guidance. You have much to learn from them. They have much to learn from each other. So, nurture the lay ministry of this place not only so they might help you grow, but also so that they are not wholly dependent upon you for their nurture. Every person here must be wholly dependent upon God alone, and then in the care of each other. When you are wholly dependent upon God, expect changes."

"Yes, Bishop Asbury. Yes, sir."

Sarah began to cry, and she wiped her eyes with a handkerchief.

"And remember, the fourth thing, find wisdom, encouragement, and renewal in fellowship with others—other clergy, other churches, locally and nationally. Clergy burn out happens when pastors lose touch with others, working so long and hard that they forget they were created to be in relationships of mutual encouragement, professionally and personally. When we connect with others in this way, expect changes."

"Yes, sir, Bishop," Allen said as he humbly lowered his head.

"Fifth, and probably most importantly, remember, this is not your ministry, and this is not your church. This is the body of Christ, and this is Christ's ministry. You must be a servant ready, willing, and able to do as Christ calls you. The minute you think otherwise, you will lose your way. Offer yourself humbly to your Lord and change will be unavoidable," said Asbury.

Allen said, "Yes, sir. I will not forget that."

Asbury walked to the front of the stage. Addressing the crowd, he said, "No successful, transformative, healthy ministry is ever a one-person show. If church and its leader are to form a partnership that is strong and enduring, you must honor each other as

Christ has already honored you. Everyone here, pastor and each individual person, is both messenger and servant one to another. Although we install Reverend Allen in the special office of bishop, called and set apart by vows of faithfulness, such vows do not set him above anyone, nor below anyone. The community of Christ is bound together in mutual service and message. You are all in this together. Given this, I also charge you with these three things as God's gathered people at Bethel with these things.

"First, expect to change. That is because the Spirit still broods over us, Christ still walks among us, and God still calls us. And you have elected Pastor Allen to help you discern God's purposes, to embark on a journey of transformation and come into closer communion with God. Change will come as your years together unfold. You will be comforted by this ministry, but you will be challenged and confronted as well.

"Second, remember that you are called together as the body of Christ for God's great purposes. Pastor Allen is not a proxy for your work. God doesn't need another fan club. God needs workers in the vineyard. Paul reminds us in Ephesians, there is one body and one Spirit and each of us was given Christian gifts. Some would be apostles, some prophets, some evangelists, some pastors and teacher, not for personal glorification but so the saints would be equipped for the work of ministry, for the building up of the body of Christ. This world, yea, this part of the world needs to know God's love and grace through each of you. This is a partnership of people and pastor on behalf of a mighty and merciful God. You are embarking on holy work."

Asbury continued, "Third, honor Bishop Allen in this ministry. While this is a partnership, there is also a peculiar setting apart that happens when someone takes ordination vows of faithfulness and accepts a call from a trusting, yearning congregation. It can be a lonely position and there is often little to go on, to know if you are making a difference. A pastor is more likely to hear the vocal complainers than the quiet supporters, and the bishop is under enormous pressure to wade into conflict with wisdom beyond human capability when it gets personal. So honor Allen's ministry. Pray for him. Give him with words of encouragement. Thank him for being your preacher, pastor, and prophet. And honor him by challenging him, asking for clarification, sharing your viewpoint. Be full and real and honest in your support."

Asbury returned to the pulpit. "The Apostle Paul frequently began his letters with wonderful words of thanksgiving, as here in his letter to the Philippians: 'I thank my God every time I remember you'—not just occasionally, but every time—'constantly praying with joy in every one of my prayers for all of you,'—constantly and for everyone—'because of your sharing in the gospel from the first day until now.' Paul goes on to say, 'I am confident of this, that the one who began a good work among you will bring it to completion by the day of Jesus Christ. It is right for me to think this way about all of you, because you hold me in your heart, for all of you share in God's grace with me....' Indeed, today affirms once again that all of you are in God's grace and are partners in the sharing of the gospel. With joy, thanksgiving, and prayer, God's good work will be manifest among you."

Asbury waited for the cheering and clapping to lessen before continuing.

"But if you give thanks for each other, honor each other, and remember that God has called you to this time and place for a reason, that God has work for you to do together, then you can be sure that there are purposeful changes ahead. Will you commit to these charges? Signify by saying 'I will.'"

"I will," the majority spoke aloud.

"Good. May you perceive it with the joy and hope that only the Spirit can give and may your years together be marked with great faithfulness. May God's blessings be on you all. Let's pray. Deacons and ministers, come lay hands on your bishop and his wife."

Several people joined them on stage. They put their hands on the neck, head, and shoulders of the Allens.

"Gracious Heavenly Father, as we commission these servants, we ask for your glory to rest on them. As a church, we have promised to hold their arms up like they did in Old Testament times. May they ever be a servant committed to your calling and mission. May your Spirit rest upon them and give them leadership and peace. In Jesus's name, we pray. Amen."

The members of the church clapped their hands and some cheered.

"And to help you remember to that you are called to be a servant, I'll ask someone to bring that tub of water, so I can wash your feet." Asbury kneeled before the now seated Allens As he dipped their feet in the water in the tub, he said, "This day, we dedicate to your service among your people, Richard and Sarah Allen. Bless them with insight, compassion, wisdom, and love as they minister to the lost, the lonely, the young, the seeking, the dying, the bereaved, the hungry, and the joyful. Deepen and enrich Richard's spiritual life until all words and deeds convey a loving spirit, a grace of understanding, and a quiet, firm, resolute witness to you as the way, the truth and the light."

Richard cried as his friend knelt before him, a white man sprinkling water over his naked black feet.

Asbury concluded his prayer by saying, "By your Holy Spirit, unite this bishop and people in a strong and holy partnership, encouraging, honoring, and loving of each other, that together they might be a witness to your glory, hope, and mercy."

Asbury stood and announced, "Ladies and gentlemen, I present to you, Bishop Richard and Lady Sarah Allen."

Chapter 22

A White Visitor

One day, Richard was with his wife in the local market, smelling the fruit waiting for hungry buyers. The peaches were pungent with flavor.

"Honey, smell this peach. It smells amazing," Richard said pushing the round fruit into his wife's nostrils.

Sarah pushed back from the fruit. "It truly does. Get some if you want. I can make a cobbler."

The couple's shopping was interrupted by a white woman carrying her basket toward them. Her basket was full of various finds—cucumbers, green peppers, and a few tomatoes.

"Excuse me, are you Reverend Allen?" she asked.

"Why, yes, I am," Allen said.

"I don't mean to bother you, but are you the one who preaches at that African peoples' church?" she asked, blushing.

"Yes, ma'am. I am he. Now, what can I do for you?"

"Oh, I heard that Reverend Asbury had been at your church recently. He is an outstanding preacher. He really speaks to me. I sure do wish I could have heard him in person," the lady gushed.

"Well, why didn't you? You most certainly could have," Richard said.

The woman shook her head. "I couldn't have. I'm white. I'm

not allowed to attend your church." She adjusted the ties of her bonnet. "Am I?"

Richard chuckled. "Why would you say that?"

"Well, I've heard you don't like white people in your space. But then I heard that Reverend Asbury had been there, so I thought I'd ask," she said.

"I don't know who told you that." Richard handed the peaches to Sarah. "I didn't get your name, ma'am?"

"My name is Esther Kelley. My brother attends St. George's Church, and he said you left because you didn't like white people."

Richard offered a small bow. "Pleasure to make your acquaintance, Esther. May I call you Esther?"

The woman nodded vigorously. "Yes, of course. Or you can call me Mrs. Kelley. Your choice."

"Alright, Esther. This is my wife, Sarah," he said, pulling Sarah into a side hug.

"Oh, hello, Sarah. Nice to meet you." Mrs. Kelley smiled warmly.

"Same to you as well, Mrs. Kelley," greeted Sarah.

Sarah had filled her basket with plenty of color. There were red apples, the orange-red peaches Richard had chosen, and some purple plums.

"My dear, Esther heard that we don't accept white people at Bethel."

Sarah turned on the woman with wide eyes. "Oh, that's not true at all. All people are welcome to our church."

"That's what I told her. We do not have respect of persons." Richard's nose flared in anger. "Our church is African in name only. For me, the spirit of the African Methodist Episcopal Church is captured by two or three words—the first is liberation, the second, development, and the third is definition. We are about the liberation of the oppressed people of the African diaspora. That is why we left St. George's. Not because we don't like those who are white."

Sarah patted her husband's arm. "We are for their development.

Call it self-help, if you will. Their development in the world and society on equal footing as everybody else."

"And third," Richard added, "that we will define ourselves and our issues. We will define our own goals because whoever makes the definition has already forecast the outcome."

Sarah smiled and took a deep breath. "I think what he means is that at Bethel we have an institution that got its start back in 1787 before black men—even before they were entirely free—striving for some sense of dignity. Those brave souls who left St. George's, and I was not there, had the courage and integrity to step out and to give leadership to what became the greatest treasures of our time."

"We emphasize justice—justice for people of every color," Richard continued. "We are Methodists believing a simple gospel of orderly rules and disciplines. We are Episcopal in that we are governed by a conference of bishops—Asbury being one. What is most important though is we are a church. Our goal is to worship God and serve the community."

"The African Methodist Episcopal Church emphasizes the importance of being a total Christian citizen in every way," Sarah added. "And what's more, in the family, we believe in Christ's teaching as guidelines as we ask God for guidance. In our church, we take part in devotions, and we join with other believers to worship God. We believe in serving our community and taking time and energy to help develop adequate neighborhoods helping people understand the political process with the goal to bring God's word to everyone. We want to use our influence and resources to help the poor and oppressed everywhere and to seek justice."

Esther's fingers fingered the bow at her throat. "Oh, I have been misled. What my brother described was that you are anti-white."

Richard shook his head. "That could not be further from the truth. We are not anti-white. We are anti-mistreatment, anti-disrespect, and anti-unequal treatment by color lines. We don't want anything special for being black—only the rights afforded white people and promised to all people by the Constititution." Richard put a hand to his chest. "I mean, how can I, a former slave, deny anyone the freedom to worship God? I remember the day the Lord shook my dungeon and the chains fell off, and he set me free." He turned to his wife and reached for the basket full of fruit. "Oh, I am sorry dear, let me take that from you. It must be getting heavy."

"I did not know you were a former slave," Mrs. Kelley admitted. "My brother just described you as an uppity colored man who did not want to worship with us whites."

"I wish you had been there that Sunday morning at St. George's to experience the foul treatment. We had already been pushed to the balcony because the church was so full and more white people had come forcing the blacks to move. We had already been segregated and the ushers tried to stop us from praying. They even had the audacity to grab my friend, Absalom Jones, from his kneeling position. He asked them to just wait until prayer was over and then he'd move, but they were adamant." Richard shook the basket in his hands to demonstrate how the ushers had pulled on the praying people. "They even enlisted some of the other white members to forcefully make us obey, but instead of submitting, we just left. That day we decided we would never return to St. George's. We decided it was our time to find a space where we could worship the Lord as we saw fit. St. George's would never be plagued by the black folks again." Richard looked Esther in her eyes. "So, in a way, your brother and those who think like him, are responsible for us having an 'all-black' church."

"Oh, my goodness. I had not heard about that. That is deplorable." Mrs. Kelley's face turned bright red. "I cannot believe they treated you like that. When I see my brother, I'm going to tell him about how he conveniently left that part out of his retelling. Ooh, this is getting heavy." Esther placed her basket onto the floor after having switched the basket between her arms several times.

"Our church aims to meet the spiritual, material, educational, and cultural needs of not solely black Americans. We encourage black independence and dignity, self-reliance, and development. I am indeed grateful to the Methodist conference who saw me and sent revivalists like Freeborn Garretson to the meeting where the Lord saved me. They taught me to read and write and schooled me and other Negroes. That's where I met my first wife in a Methodist school. I am indebted to the Methodists. Where would I be had it not been for the providence of God and his guidance?"

He wiped the wetness from his eyes, not aware he had been crying until then.

"Oh, I'm sorry. I always get choked up when I tell that story," he said.

"Nothing to apologize for. It's a tale that needs retelling," said Esther. "I'm honored to hear it." She wiped her eyes with a handkerchief she had removed from her bag.

"Perhaps you would be interested in attending an upcoming service as my special guest?" Richard suggested. "You and your brother. I believe you will find our church welcoming to you. We are committed to ecumenicalism promoting equal justice for every class and color. We highly support decent living standards for all. I think you will find our commitment to Christian consciousness where we place emphasis on Christian living in our everyday life especially enlightening. I think you will find our church has been designed to meet the special needs of black people in this time of slavery and oppression, but we wish to be part of a community which embraces all people who have submitted their lives to God and who serve Christ with their full hearts, minds, and souls." Richard smiled at her.

"I may just take you up on your invitation." She smiled back. "Thank you, Pastor. Don't be surprised if you look up from the pulpit and you see my whole family sitting there. I do doubt my brother will join us though." She extended her hand to him. "Reverend, it was an honor to meet you."

"A pleasure indeed, Mrs. Kelley." He shook her hand firmly. "If you don't mind, Sarah and I are going to finish our shopping now."

"Oh, yes, I should do the same." Esther picked up her basket from the floor and hung it from her right arm. With a quick wave and a smile, she walked past them into the fruit aisle.

"That was nice, wasn't it, Richard?" Sarah asked as Esther moved away.

Richard nodded. "I hope she takes us up on our invitation. There are probably many others who feel the same way and question our existence. We should do more in the way of grassroots community education." He foisted their shopping basket further onto his arm and held up a large, white vegetable with a center stalk. "Do you know how to cook this?"

"No, I don't. I don't even know what that is," Sarah said turning up her nose at the find.

"Well, I know you know what to do with these," Richard said, holding up a yam.

Chapter 23

PAS Challenge

The sun had risen high into the morning sky. Richard had been alone in his study drinking coffee deep in his thoughts. Sarah entered in her gray housecoat, the belt tightened around her waist.

"Dear, can I freshen your coffee? A little fill-up?" Sarah held the coffee pot in her hand with a cloth.

Richard looked in his coffee mug. "Sure, I'll take a refill. Thank you." As Sarah refilled the mug, he asked, "Do we have more milk?"

"I believe there is some in the ice box. I'll get it," Sarah said as she exited and went back into the kitchen area. A moment later, she called out, "Dear heart, I think we might need some more ice today. Do you think you could send for some?"

"Yes, I'll get the errand boy to go down to the ice man and order the ice. I'll tell him to bring the order later today."

Sarah came back into the room with a small bottle of milk. After pouring some into his mug, she stepped back and assessed her husband.

"Dear husband, what seems to be on your mind? You seem so deep in your thoughts this morning. Is something bothering you?"

"Nothing, really."

"Richard, I know you. I know when something is bothering you. What is it?" Sarah pushed.

He laughed. "You know me so well." He sighed deeply. "Of a truth, dear wife, I am troubled some. I have just been wondering, am I doing enough?"

"What has brought this on? Are there troubles at the church?" Sarah raised her eyebrows.

"No. I just wonder if there is any more I should be doing?" Richard blew heavily into his coffee cup and sipped afterwards.

"What bothers you so now?" Sarah asked as she sat next to him.

"Everyone knows I am against slavery. That's not even a matter of discussion. I preach against it regularly and am an outspoken combatant. I want to end slavery. Now. It's a terrible bolt against our country. It must be stopped by any means." Richard slapped the table in anger, scattering the pens atop it.

"Yes, I agree wholeheartedly. It really is a stain," Sarah agreed.

"I have been fasting and praying, and I came across this passage of scripture in Isaiah 58 verse six." He held out the family Bible for Sarah to read see.

"Is not this the fast that I have chosen? to loosen the bands of wickedness, to undo the heavy burdens, and to let the oppressed go free, and that ye break every yoke?"

Richard looked into his wife's eyes.

"I should be doing more. It may not be enough to be vocal and preach against slavery. Maybe I need to put my hatred into action. Maybe I'm not doing enough." He wiped tears from his eyes.

"Oh, Richard." Sarah kissed his forehead. "Don't cry. How much more do you think you should be doing?"

"Preaching and teaching may not be enough. Maybe it is time that I—we—get into the fray. Put some action to all this … this talk." Richard pushed his Bible aside. "I've been talking with some members of the Pennsylvania Abolition Society who say they do not have enough colored people to help in their efforts. Their latest report stated, 'too many blacks are either brought up under the control of parents just emerged from slavery whose weaknesses they entail upon them.' They say that the cause of emancipation is weakening. And those people were my steadfast allies."

"What does that mean though?" Sarah seemed confused.

"It means that not enough black people are getting involved with abolition. It could be their satisfaction with 'gradual abolition' rather than immediate," Richard said.

"That I can understand. People want freedom now. Not tomorrow or whenever," Sarah said.

"Not every master was like Master Sturgis who would allow me an opportunity to purchase my freedom. What's more is I have even had to defend myself against whites who have said I have turned my back to the cause of freedom," Richard said.

"Well, have you?"

"Absolutely not. The Bible is not saying eventually. Read here. It's also in Isaiah 58. This time it is verses seven through thirteen."

Sarah took the family Bible from Richard's hands and read as instructed.

Sarah read aloud. "'Is it not to deal thy bread to the hungry, and that thou bring the poor that are cast out to thy house? When thou seest the naked, that thou cover him; and that thou hide not thyself from thine own flesh? Then shall thy light break forth as the morning, and thine health shall spring forth speedily: and thy righteousness shall go before thee; the glory of the Lord shall be thy reward. Then shalt thou call, and the Lord shall answer; thou shalt cry, and he shall say, Here I am. If thou take away from the midst of thee the yoke, the putting forth of the finger, and speaking vanity; And if thou draw out thy soul to the hungry, and satisfy the afflicted soul; then shall thy light rise in obscurity, and thy darkness be as the noon day: And the Lord shall guide thee continually, and satisfy thy soul in drought, and make fat thy bones: and thou shalt be like a watered garden, and like a spring of water, whose waters fail not. And they that shall be of thee shall build the old waste places: thou shalt raise up the foundations of many generations;

and thou shalt be called, The repairer of the breach, The restorer of paths to dwell in. If thou turn away thy foot from the sabbath, from doing thy pleasure on my holy day; and call the sabbath a delight, the holy of the Lord, honorable; and shalt honour him, not doing thine own ways, nor finding thine own pleasure, nor speaking thine own words.'"

Sarah frowned. "Fasting does all this?"

"Yes. These are the resultant blessings of a fast that is honorable to the Lord. Furthermore, that's what I feel the Lord calling me to. He wants me to get involved more. To get involved with those who are seeking freedom. To get my hands dirty. The Lord has truly blessed us, but we can't forget the depths from which we have come," said Richard. "We have been financially blessed, but there are those who have escaped slavery and have made their way to Philadelphia that we need to help. To provide for even to provide some of our resources. Imagine coming to Philadelphia with nothing and being expected to be responsible for surviving. We've got this big, old house with plenty of rooms to put people in, if need be, right?"

"Richard, are you talking about helping escaped slaves? They are fugitives. Isn't that against the law? Isn't it our job as Christians to always obey the law?"

"Not if it is an unjust law. Slavery itself breaks all kinds of laws. God is calling us to a higher level of responsibility. In fact, Jesus himself broke all kinds of laws while doing his earthly ministry."

Richard paused before explaining. "When he interacted with the woman with the issue of blood. When she touched the hem of Jesus's garment, that made him ceremonially unclean and according to Jewish law, he was supposed to be cast out of the city. Then when he went to Jairus's house, he should have been disbarred from service for being near to a dead body."

"Then, as always, we need to do what the Lord says. Even if the children and I must tighten up to allow space for the visitors," Sarah agreed.

"Yes, ma'am. That is what we will do then. Together we will provide uplift to an already broken-down black populace. Whatever we must do, whether it's at this private home or our home in the country or our other rental properties, we will give room to break down the walls, barriers, and obstacles to our strangers and make them friends. Amen?"

"Amen, preacher," Sarah said in agreement.

"I have a story to tell. I've gone from slave to free, from slave to trader and grocer, from slave to master chimney sweep, from master chimney sweep to dry goods dealer, to minister and now property owner aimed to help escaped, fugitive slaves. Yes, God has been good to me. And I will obey," Richard said with surety.

Over the next period of years, Richard enlisted the Bethel church family into his plans. They bought several other properties around and near the church. These properties would fit well into the plan to both secure his economic footprint, but to ensure there would be space to provide housing for new Philadelphians. Sarah would be regaled as the "Mother of Bethel" as she provided food and nourishment to the travelers. Sarah made sure her home was never shut against the friendless, the homeless, or the penniless.

Chapter 24

FUGITIVE AID

Slavery,'" Richard read a pamphlet aloud, "'is such an atrocious debasement of human nature, that at its very extirpation, if not performed with solicitous care, may sometimes open a source of serious evils.' "Well, Benjamin Franklin and I have not much in common given his identity as a former slaveowner, but he is correct here when he warns '… under such circumstances, freedom may often prove a misfortune to former slaves and prejudicial to society,'" Richard said to his friend, William. "I have said, contrary to Franklin, to allay whites' fear of black equality, if only whites would simply believe in their own Christian language and liberate blacks, teach them scripture, and the principles of good citizenship, and watch them become pious and respectable members of the American republic."

"You are right about that," Jones said. "What is Franklin worried about? Give blacks freedom and they'll just run amuck throughout society like brutes?"

"Of a truth, if you love your children, if you love your country, if you love the God of love, clean your hands from slaves, burden not your children or country with them," Richard said defiantly.

"This country needs to repent for slavery and fast," William agreed.

"I am committed to calling for us to humiliate ourselves and pray. The Bible declares that those who are the called should 'humble themselves, pray, and seek my face' then God will forgive their sins and heal their land." Allen sat forward to make his point. "It's interesting you feel that way. You know the abolition folks say they need more blacks to help in the cause—they say we're losing the emancipation battle—unless more of us get involved."

"Oh, I'm involved already. Just learned of a man who ran from slavery in Alabama and is looking for housing," William said.

"All the way from Alabama? My Lord, he's come a long way," Richard said, stroking his chin. "Where is he? I'd love to meet him and talk to him about his journey."

"I'll bring him to you tonight. He only moves at night," said William.

"That makes sense. Bring him by the house and we'll talk about his options," said Allen.

Later that evening, Richard paced in his living room. He had lit two candles while he waited. Sarah had food warming in the kitchen to serve the visitor.

"Dear, where is William? The food is getting cold," Sarah said.

"I am sure they are on their way. Apparently, this man William is bringing has been on the run for months. I suspect he does not trust many people he encounters. Wait … What is that?" Richard listened out the window. "Maybe that's them."

Richard carried a lantern toward the rear door. The lantern illuminated two dark shapes on the porch—William and a dark-skinned man in dirty overalls.

Richard ushered them into his home and shut the door tight.

"Reverend Allen, this here is Marvin," William presented the stranger.

"Oh, I told you, ere'body calls me Paw Paw," Marvin scolded.

"Reverend, I'm honored to meet you, sir," Marvin said as he removed his hat.

"Oh, the pleasure is mine, good sir. And this here is my wife, Sarah," Richard opened his arm to present his wife.

"So nice to make your acquaintance. Welcome. Are you hungry?" Sarah pointed toward the dining room table which had been set formally.

"Oh, yes'em. I could eat a horse, I reckin'," Marvin said.

"Well, come on and have a seat. I've got some ham hocks and beans. Eat as much as you want," Sarah invited.

"Oh, my. Thank you kindly." Marvin sat at the fine table and began to cry.

"What's wrong? There's no need to cry," Sarah reasoned.

"Oh, I's sorry. I ain't et like dis for a munt since I left Alabama. I been eatin' bugs and lizards I foun' in de woods. It be nice to eat real food. Thank ye, ma'am. Uh, kin I have sum of dat dere cohnbread?"

Richard passed the pan with cornbread. Marvin immediately crumbled it atop the beans and mixed it all together.

Suddenly, he stopped and looked down at his hands. "I's sohhry. I shoulda wash my hands fihrs fo' I set down to eat. It jes' all look so good an' smell good too. Smell like home."

Sarah passed the man the plate of ham hocks next, then the beans, piling it all up before him. "Oh, never you mind. I just want you to eat. That's what it's for. And save room for dessert. I've got an apple pie cooling in the window when you're ready."

"Tank ya," Marvin said, his mouth full.

Richard eyed Marvin's arms in the candlelight. They were scarred and had bled at some time. He bore a reminder on the side of his neck of a battle.

"You look like you have been through it," Richard said, staring at the man.

"Richard, remember your manners. That was rude," Sarah scolded.

"No need for 'pologies. I mus' look a fright. I's 'fraid I did have a goin roun' wif sum thohns an' briahs as I ran through de swamp. I stay low in de woods fo' weeks. Dem creeks be col'," Marvin said. "I slep' on de groun'. Too bad dem red fihe ants dinna want me sleepin' on dey spot. Lawd Jesus, dey lit into me sumpin' awful. I came cross'd a watah moccasin near de creek bed. I saw dis black-berrh bush, an' I try to reach it when he snap't at me."

"Oh, my goodness," Sarah cried, clutching her necklace. "What did you do?"

Marvin pointed his fork across the table. "I poke at it wif a stick an it ran away. Dey mo' skirred o' you dan you is of it." He speared another bite of ham hock and shoved it into his mouth full of half missing teeth.

Sarah frowned. "I don't think that's true." She began cleaning up as the men cleaned off their plates.

"You sed sumpin 'bout sum apple pie, right?" Marvin inquired when she took away his plate.

Sarah chuckled. "That I did. I'll get you a slice."

"And ma'am," Marvin asked, "kin I ask you fo' a cup of tea if it's not too much trubble?"

"No trouble at all. I just need to boil some water. You want your pie first?" Sarah asked.

"I think I kin wait. I'll have my tea wif de pie, thank ye," Marvin said, "I'll let dis meal set down in my belly. Lawd ham muhsy, dat was *mmm-mmm* good." Marvin rubbed his stomach and sighed.

"Alright, I will bring that right back," Sarah said and exited the room, singing a tune as she went.

"O worship the King all-glorious above,
 O gratefully sing his power and his love:
Our shield and defender, the Ancient of Days,
 pavilioned in splendor and girded with praise."

"She has the voice of an angel. Jes beautifuh." Marvin closed his eyes as he listened to Sarah sing.

"Yes, she does. I make her sing at church sometimes," Richard said smiling.

Sarah reentered the dining room and placed a white saucer with a heaping helping of apple pie in front of her guest. "Here you are, Marvin. You want one lump or two in your tea?"

"Two, please and thank ye," Marvin said.

He picked up his fork again and shoveled a big bite into his mouth, then continued his story.

"I thought I was a gonah too. I wrassle a nine-foot gater. It was a biggun. I was duckin' in de watah coz I saw a patty rollah. I jump'd in de Polecat Creek. I saw it cummin fo' me. Lucky, I had ole' Bessie wit' me." He pulled out a large silver knife from his waistband. "He came at me, and I stuck 'im with Bessie blade heah, and dat was dat. He ain' bodda me no mo'. I cook'd him fo' dinnah." Marvin smiled, showing gaps in his teeth and bits of apple pie still clinging to what teeth remained.

"Oh, you ate an alligator." Sarah cringed. "What did it taste like?"

"A bit like chicken," said Marvin.

Just then, the Allens' young son, Richard Jr, wandered into the dining room. "What tastes like chicken?"

"Oh, Mr. Marvin was telling us how he ate an alligator," Sarah said, pulling him into her arms.

"*Ewww*, an alligator? For real? A real live alligator with the tough green skin?" the little boy made a face.

"And who is dis fine youngin'?" Marvin asked.

"This is our son, Richard Jr. He's going to be a preacher like his father, right, son?" Sarah beamed down at her child.

"Dat's good. You gon' be a right, good preacha, I betcha," Marvin said. "How ole is he?"

"He's six. He's our oldest. There's Richard Jr., James, John, Peter, Sara, and Ann. He should be in bed like his brothers and sisters." Sarah patted her son's bottom and directed him back out of the room. "Mr. Marvin will be here in the morning when you wake."

"Call me, Paw Paw. All my kin call me Paw Paw," Marvin said.

"Good night, Mister Paw Paw." Richard Jr. yawned as he walked out of the room.

"Oh, I'm sorry, Paw Paw. I didn't even ask you if you planned to stay the night. I just assumed you were," Sarah said.

"Yes, please stay. That way in the morning we can strategize about what your plans are now that you've made your way to Philadelphia," Richard said.

"Dat's simple. I hope to mek enuf money to send fo' my wife an' chillun," said Marvin.

"Oh, how many children do you have?" Sarah asked.

"Sebben, dey all in chains in Alabammy," Marvin confided.

A moment of silence reigned over the table. William and Richard shared a pointed glance.

Sarah yawned and rose from the table. "I'm going to turn in now. What would you like for breakfast, Paw Paw? I was planning pancakes and eggs."

"Oh, yes ma'am. Dat soun' righteous. Do you all have a cow for milk? I kin earn my keep," Marvin said.

"Oh, no sir, you are our guest," said Richard. "You don't have to work. It's our duty."

"I's ret for bed mysef then. Do you min'?" Marvin yawned.

Richard nodded. "Do you mind if we pray for you first before we all turn in? Sarah, can you hold on a moment?" Richard stood and put his hand on Marvin's shoulder. "We believe in the laying on of hands. Is that alright with you?"

"Yessuh. Go 'head." Marvin bowed his head.

"C'mon, Brother William. Join us, please."

The trio surrounded Marvin and offered praise and prayer to their Lord God, then William went back to his home and the others retired for the evening.

Chapter 25

Elias Hicks

Sarah, listen to this…" Richard leaned forward at his desk. "I've been reading *Observations on the Slavery of Africans and Their Descendants*. The author Elias Hicks advocates a consumer boycott of products by slaves." Richard cheered as he read. "Listen. 'It would doubtless have a particular effect on the slave holders, by circumscribing their avarice, and preventing their heaping up riches, and living in a state of luxury and excess on the gain of oppression,'" Richard said smiling.

"This is just the energy that our abolitionist movement needs. It has been stagnant for a while," Sarah confirmed.

"I agree. It is time that we, as a nation, put an embargo on trading on the backs of slaves. It is 1818, after all. We have had slavery since 1619. It's time for it to end, and this will put a life tax on goods produced by slaves. Perhaps slaveowners will not like paying the tax?" Richard said.

"A *life tax*? I like the sound of that." Sarah smiled.

"I'm going to go down to the church. Let me get myself together." Richard slowly stood from his chair and reached for his walking stick leaning against the desk. "These old knees just don't want to move as quickly as my mind wants them to," Richard said. "Oh, come on, Arthur-itis, I've got things to do."

"Take your time, honey. Arthritis has taken its toll on you," Sarah said, holding out her arms to aid and support.

"I'll be alright. Just takes a little longer to get around."

Richard hobbled down the street. As he neared the church, he eyed Whipper's, a black-owned grocery store and decided to stop in.

"Good morning, Mr. Whipper. It's a lovely day, is it not?" Richard called to the owner, Whipper, who was dusting some shelves.

"Oh, good morning, Pastor. A lovely day, indeed," Whipper said.

"How goes it?" Richard replied.

"You know, just like I always say, education, temperance, economy, and universal liberty. That's how we black folks are going to come up in this world." Whipper leaned against a shelf.

"Yes, sir." Richard chuckled. "We are on the come up for sure. Say, have you heard about the calling from Elias Hicks who wants folks to boycott slave-produced goods?" Richard asked.

"Heard of it? I have been a free goods dealer for a long time. Nothing in this store has been produced by slaves." Whipper held out his arms and spun around displaying his wares. "In fact, I am a member of the Free Produce Society, an organization run by the Quakers out of Delaware. We refuse any products that come from slave labor. It's the only way to put slavery to an end in this country," Whipper said. "It's time to cripple the slaveowners."

"You are saying the right things, sir. Talking my language. Do you mind if I have one of these grapes?"

"No, go right ahead. For as much as you have done for this community, I think a grape is a small pittance. In fact, have a handful," offered Whipper.

Richard took a handful of the deep purple globes.

Whipper continued, "I wonder if I could propose something to you?"

"Sure. Go right ahead," said Richard, then popped a grape in his mouth.

"Well, you and Reverend Jones were part of the leadership starting your own black church, right?"

"That is correct," Allen said smiling.

"Well, I am wondering if you all can do the same thing for the Free Produce movement. We need a black people's effort," said Whipper.

"The Quakers aren't doing right by you?"

"They have been fine, but they just don't get it all the time. I bring situations and concerns to them, but they just don't get it. I'm always having to justify myself. Sometimes, I just want my opinion to be accepted without questioning," Whipper answered.

Richard rubbed his chin. "I understand. I have been with my well-meaning white Methodist brethren who many still don't understand why we left St. George's and started our own. What you are describing is little different from what we did with the Free African Society. How's this? A Colored Free Produce Society of Pennsylvania?"

"I love it! Can you make it happen?" Whipper smiled and hugged Richard. "This is great news because the Free Produce Society is coming to Philadelphia to host their annual conference soon. I can introduce you to our leader, Mr. Thomas M'Clintock. Maybe you can broach the need for the Colored Free Produce Society? I hear that Francis Ellen Watkins has been invited to speak. She has been an outspoken and deeply committed advocate of the freedom movement. She always says she would gladly pay more for a free labor dress," said Whipper.

"I'd love to hear her speak. She has been a loud voice in the antislavery movement," Richard said as he continued snacking on grapes. His thoughts turned to Jarena Lee and how he could learn from Ms. Watkins' leadership.

Richard continued. "I think we have a plan. We'll introduce the idea to Mr. M'Clintock and begin to organize around for a colored version of the Free Produce Society. You know, as I think about it, you could really draw in local business by advertising as a free grocery. I do think people would like that."

"Whipper's Free Grocery? I like that too. Aren't you just full of good ideas?" said Whipper. "It was nice talking to you, Pastor. You have given me much to think about."

"Yes, indeed. And thank you for the grapes." Richard exited the store and went next door to the church. He was amazed to see William there.

"My brother, my brother, it is good to see you. I hadn't seen much of you since we helped Paw Paw," greeted Richard.

"I am the same man I have always been. I'm still your brother— still committed to the struggle," said William.

"I'm glad. You and I have been called into service again," Richard said.

"Again? How? By whom?" asked William.

"You know Mr. Whipper next door?"

"Whipper, the grocer? Yes, I know him. Why?"

"He has a brilliant idea, and he would like our help pulling it all together. He wants to start a colored people's organization focusing on free labor. It is poised to ignite the abolitionists' fire that is so needed today," said Richard.

"Anything that is helpful to the antislavery cause—count me in." William clapped his hands.

"He is involved in the Free Produce Society, and they are formed to eschew products made by slave labor. He wants to create a colored version where he will not have to justify his existence," Richard said.

"You mean like we did with Bethel? We needed to throw off that servile fear, that the habit of oppression and bondage trained us up in," said William.

"Yes, just like that. White folks don't get how their words are so oppressive. They just expect us to fold up and submit to their every whim," said Richard.

"And they are so scared of a free black society. They imagine blacks are going to run rampant and take over. What I really feel is that they worry that we'll treat them the same way they've treated us," Jones argued.

"I concur. You get no argument from me," Richard said as he reached out to shake Absalom's hand.

"Whipper wants you and me to meet and talk with Thomas M'Clintock about the needs of black store owners like himself," said Richard. "He's coming to Philadelphia soon."

"Anything. Yes. I'll do it. How is Marvin getting along?" William asked about Paw Paw.

"Oh, I didn't tell you? He's gone. We passed him along going North. We got the sense the authorities were searching for him, so we connected with some friends and saw him on. Last I saw him, I waved at him from the rear of a ship headed for New York. You know, the Fugitive Slave Act and all. I hope he has fared well." Richard's gaze wandered to the window.

"Maybe it's time to call more black leaders together? We've all been doing good things, but we've been siloed. No sense in doing everything alone, right?" William appealed to Richard.

"*Hmm*, that's something to think about. You're right. There's no sense in every man expending energy with solitary ideas."

Chapter 26

CALL FOR REVIVAL

One summer evening, Richard dressed as if he were going to church. "It's an important community event, right?" he said to no one in particular.

He and Sarah had noticed a sign promoting a community rally earlier that day on a local bulletin board. Richard had felt the desire to attend. He was, after all, a member of the community.

Arriving fifteen minutes late, Richard could hear the crowd cheering inside the tent. He felt very conspicuous as he marched down the aisle to a seat in the rear of the tent. As he walked from the front of the chrowd having entered from the rear, he noticed the angry eyes of the crowd following his every move.

"What is he doing here?" he thought he heard someone say.

Still another voice argued, "He doesn't belong here."

Richard thought to himself about the numerous times he'd be told he didn't belong to a society. He steeled himself as he sat in an empty seat.

A short, stocky white man stood at the lectern on the stage.

"The blacks have no place in free society. There are many who argue the illegitimacy of the African slave trade. They argue against the practice, but I believe, and I'm not alone in my thinking, that blacks are not really human. Even the Declaration of Independence confirms they're only three-fifths human. That sounds like a monster, doesn't it?"

Many attending began to clap … except those near Richard who stared in his direction instead.

"You only need to go to the ninth chapter of Genesis if you want proof. Canaan, Noah's son, was to be Japheth's servant. Ham, Noah's darker son, was to be held in a state of abject bondage. There are countless other times in the Old Testament which describe the condition of the slave. Have you heard of Abraham and Sarah and her servant Hagar? Hagar had run away from her mistress, but the angel of the Lord told her to go back to her mistress. That is in Genesis chapter fifteen. God himself cosigned having slaves. Listen to what he said to Moses when he gave the law on Mount Sinai." The speaker flipped through the pages of his Bible. "He said we should not covet thy neighbor's house, his wife or his manservant or his maidservant. Those are slaves." The man began to pace now as he talked.

This man is controverting the scriptures.

Richard leaned to the man seated next to him and questioned, "Do you know who that man is? What is his name? I arrived late after he started."

"That's Thornton Stringfellow. He's a Baptist preacher from the South. He's telling the truth of the Word. We need to hear this kind of preaching up here in the Northern states."

"*Hmm…*" Richard turned back to the speaker with a scowl.

"Joseph was a Hebrew slave who had served the Pharaoh well. He had been rewarded for good service. How far the hand of God was in the overthrow of liberty, I will not decide, but from the fact that he has singled out one of the greatest slaveholders of that age, as the object of his special favor, it would seem that the institution was one furnishing great opportunities to exercise grace and glorify God, as it still does, where its duties are faithfully discharged!"

The audience cheered Stringfellow's words as they jumped to their feet.

Richard folded his arms in anger and refused to stand.

"I could go on, but you should be convinced of God's position. Our next speakers will spell out how slavery has benefitted us financially, in our government, and our society as a whole."

More speakers? More of this nonsense? I think that's enough for me. Richard decided to exit after Stringfellow left the stage. He dipped his head and ducked out amid the cheering crowd.

Richard found his wife changing the baby's diaper in the nursery when he returned.

"How was the rally?" Sarah asked.

"I really don't want to talk about it right now," Richard said before holing up in his study where he fell on his knees and began to pray silently.

After some time, he heard his wife enter the room. He finished his prayer and stood.

"Do you want to talk about it now?" Sarah asked.

"I am sick of what is happening in the American church!" Richard began to pace as the speaker from earlier had done. "We have a disease in the church. I am sick of hate, division, and racism! We are building different altars. They are standing at their altar, and we are standing at our altar, and we have the audacity to ask God to move on our altar." Richard stopped in front of his wife. "Let me give you some Bible. In first Kings chapter eighteen, Israel was divided into two kingdoms, the northern kingdom was Israel, and the southern kingdom was Judah."

Sarah nodded. "Yes, I know."

"I know you do, but let me remind you, that he healed the altar of God. That means that he went back to the place where the church was one body. The way the Lord intended. We were never meant to have a black church, nor they a white church. He called us to be one—'one Lord, one faith, and one baptism.' We have allowed the spirit of division to take over." Here, he paused and wiped his hand over his face. "And I'm guilty. I've allowed myself to be blinded by hatred and by the hurt from my brothers at St. George's to cloud my thinking. We need a revival of kindness."

"A revival of kindness?" Sarah repeated.

"Yes. The spirit of God wants to baptize our churches with his spirit and that will necessitate us bearing kingdom fruit. When the spirit of the Lord comes upon us, we will see a production of fruit. The Bible says in the Book of Ephesians chapter 5, 'But the fruit of the spirit is love, joy, peace, longsuffering, gentleness, goodness faith, meekness, and temperance.' We need a revival of those in our church," said Richard.

"Are you saying we do not need to be an African Episcopal Methodist church any longer?"

Richard shook his head and began to pace again. "No, that's not what I am saying at all. I'm saying some things we need to let go of—like holding on to the pain of the past, like learning to see God in the face of our white brethren. There is only one kingdom!" He pointed one of his fingers to the sky.

"Then you need to make that plain to the church," said Sarah, her hands folded over her lap as she sat.

"Wait one minute." Richard walked out of the room and returned with his fishing pole. "When I go fishing, if I want to catch bass, I know what bait to use. If I want catfish, there's a different bait. When Jesus taught the disciples, he told them to 'cast their nets on the other side.' When you fish with a net, you catch whatever comes in. And the Lord told me the bait I should be using is love. I need to love through the hurt, through the pain—love even those who rejected us and condemned us for being black. Jesus said, 'by this will men know you are my disciples, that you have love for one another.' God is about to heal a divided church in America! He's about to help us get back together," said Richard.

"Well, I guess that community rally inspired something in you." Sarah smiled.

"Yes. The Lord convicted my heart. I think he is calling out to us to lead the charge with love. He's looking for people to cast their nets far and wide."

On the following Sunday, Richard barely allowed the praise service to conclude before he approached the pulpit. Among many scriptures, he referenced Acts chapter one, verse eight.

"'But ye shall receive power, after that the Holy Ghost is come upon you. And ye shall be witnesses unto me in Jerusalem, and in all Judea, and in Samaria, and to the uttermost part of the earth.' That means it is time to go fishing, my friends," he told his congregation. "In the gospels, Jesus told his disciples to cast their nets on the other side. Now, these men were professional fishermen who had been toiling all night long, and here comes Jesus telling them to do it another way." Pastor Allen waited for some of the murmurs to die down before continuing. "That means maybe they don't look like you, maybe they don't dress like you, but they still need Jesus."

"Amen. That's right," a female parishioner yelled.

"We need a revival of love, joy, peace, and kindness. What we need is a good old-fashioned move of the Holy Ghost where hearts are changed, minds are renewed, and where people receive love."

"Yes sir. You better preach!" another woman yelled.

"So, what am I saying?" Richard looked out over those gathered. "It's harvest time. Harvest time, my friends. That means you need to invite someone to church next week. Not your ordinary friends, but someone who doesn't quite fit your usual suspect. No, don't just invite them to church. Invite them to the kingdom of God. Go out into the 'highways and hedges' and compel them to come." He slapped his hand on the pulpit. "Do you know what compel means? Let me show you." Richard descended the stage and grabbed his son, Richard Jr., by the scruff of the neck and pushed him around the front of the church. "See, that's compelling them. Don't accept any excuses. Push, pull, drag them here if you must. That is what God is expecting of you."

"Yes, sir. I will do it!" a man in a dark suit agreed.

"As we leave today, I want you to get a picture in your mind of someone who needs to meet Jesus. I'm going to pray that God gives you an opportunity to invite them." Richard then lead the congregation in prayer. He prayed for divine kingdom opportunities and strength and boldness for his congregation.

Chapter 27

Family Sing-along

Oh, honey. That meal was wonderful. You truly outdid yourself," Richard said.

"Thank you, dear heart. It was really nothing special—just some cube steak, mashed potatoes, and corn," Sarah said as she wiped her mouth with a napkin.

"It was still good though. Sara, will you wash the dishes, please?" Richard asked their teenage daughter.

"Why do I always have to wash the dishes? Why can't Ann do them sometimes? Or Richard Jr., or James, or Peter? The boys never have to do them!" Sara whined. "It's just not fair."

"It's not fair that your mother cooks for us every day either, but you sit at this table and partake of her hard-earned work," Richard said.

Richard Jr. laughed. "She surely shovels that food into her mouth, doesn't she? And never offers to help our mother."

"Go on, dear. It might not seem fair, but this is the plight of womenkind. The boys help with other chores," Richard's wife answered. "Women must cook and clean. That's just the way things are."

"Yes, ma'am," Sara said, scooting her chair back from the table.

"And Peter and Richard Jr., you two can clear the table," their mother commanded.

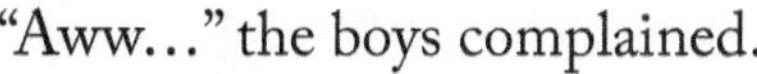

"Aww…" the boys complained.

"Do as your mother said, boys, and without making a fuss," Richard added.

"Yes, sir," the boys said at the same time, each grabbing some dishes from the table. They carried the dirty dishes into the kitchen and slammed them near their sister.

"Here, missy," Peter said.

"Mom!" Sara cried. "Peter is being mean."

"No, I am not. That's just Sara acting like a spoiled brat," Peter said.

"Quit whining, Sara. We all have our appointed chores. Yours just happens to be dishes. I don't hear you complaining when I must take the trash out," Richard Jr. said.

Sara made ready a fire to begin heating the water all the while complaining, "Washing dishes, washing dishes, that's all I ever do." She repeated that phrase several times.

Soon, her father entered the kitchen, interrupting her by singing.

"*Hush, do do do. Hush, do do do,*" Richard sang. "*Somebody's calling my name.*"

"Dad, cut it out," Sara said, sensing he was joking. "It's not fair."

"*Hush, do do do. Hush, do do do.*" He mimicked the bass drum. "*Somebody's calling my name.*"

Her volume increased. "Dad!"

"*Hush, do do do. Hush, do do do. Somebody's calling my name.*"

"Daddy! Stop it."

Her brothers pounded on the table in rhythm of the song.

Richard continued, "*Oh my Lord, oh my Lord. What shall I do?*"

Soon, both parents were standing in the kitchen singing, "*Hush, do do do. Hush, do do do. Somebody's calling my name.*"

The boys carried dirty plates and cups and silverware. Sara took them and washed them in the sink.

James carried a serving plate with the brown meat as he sang, "*I met my mother the other day.*"

Richard Jr. came around the corner with the bowls of corn and mashed potato remnants, singing the next verse. "*I gave her my right hand to shake.*"

James added, mimicking a baritone voice, "*And just as soon as my back was turned. She scandalized my name.*"

From the sink, Sara gave in and sang, "*Well, do you call that a mother?*"

Her young brother, John, appeared singing, "*No, no. Well, do you call that a mother?*"

Sarah sang in response while smiling, "*No, child, no.*"

Their father placed a hand on his chest and belted out, "*Because she … she scandalized my name.*"

The family members joined in laughter.

Peter sang while clapping the tune, "*Have you got good religion?*"

Richard Jr. responded, "*Certainly, Lord.*"

Ann repeated, "*Have you got good religion?*"

This time Sarah responded, "*Certainly, Lord.*"

Richard sang, "*Have you been baptized?*"

Their mother answered, "*Certainly, Lord, Certainly, certainly certainly, Lord.*"

Peter asked, feigning a deep baritone, "*Do you feel like shouting?*"

The children joined in together and with loud voices, "*Certainly, Lord, Certainly, certainly, certainly, Lord!*"

James began a new song, melding it into the first. "*We are climbing Jacob's ladder. We are climbing Jacob's ladder, ladder.*"

"*We are climbing Jacob's ladder. Soldiers of the cross,*" Richard joined his son.

His wife sang, "*Ev'ry round goes higher and higher. Ev'ry round goes higher and higher, Children of the cross.*"

Sara sang to her brother Peter, "*Brother, do you love my Jesus?*"

Peter responded, "*Certainly, Lord.*"

They fell into a fit of laughter, then turned back to their chores.

"I love that song. You could almost make up lyrics for it," Sara said wringing out the dishrag in the sink. "This was fun. Y'all should sing with me every time I wash dishes. Makes the time go faster."

Richard Jr. responded in song, "*No, child, no.*"

His parents laughed aloud.

Richard answered, "*Do Lord. Do Lord. Lord, remember me.*"

His wife put her arm around his waist and answered, "*Do Lord, oh, do Lord. Lord, remember me. Way beyond the blue.*"

Richard kissed her temple and smiled. "It's important to remember, instead of complaining, just sing praises to the Lord. You'll finish in no time. Remember what the Bible says, 'Weeping may endure for the night, but joy cometh in the morning.'"

"Dad, you gotta turn everything into a sermon. Can't we simply sing as a family without you preaching at us?" Peter complained.

"Peter, my boy, I'm a preacher. What else do you expect?" Richard said before once again delving into song. "*You've got to praise him. Rise, shine. Give God the glory. Rise and shine and give God the glory. Children of the Lord.* Sing it with me, Son."

Peter sang in reply, "*Do you think I'll make a good soldier, soldier?*"

Richard answered, "*Yes, I think you will make a good soldier, soldier. Yes, I think you'll make a good soldier, soldier.*" Richard paused his singing to wrap his arms around his son. "You see, Peter, I can't help praising my Jesus. I'm reminded of the day he saved me. I know I've told you this story, but the day Christ found me, I had cried to the Lord both day and night. Suddenly, my dungeon shook, my chains flew off, and glory to God, I cried."

"Yes, you have told me all that before. And I, for one, will never get tired of hearing how God brought you out of slavery and set you free," said Peter, hugging his father tight.

"Good. Because I will never get tired of telling that story." Richard quieted then sang in a low baritone, "*No more auction block for me. No more, no more. No more auction block for me, many thousand gone. No more peck of corn for me and no more driver's lash for me.*"

"And Master Sturgis came to know the Lord because of you, right, Dad?" Richard Jr. asked.

"Yes, sir. That's why I am a preacher now. I learned the Lord wanted to use me to save others," said Richard. "I became an iterant preacher after and started traveling to preach the gospel." Richard's eyes dazzled above his flat nose and dimpled chin. "You know, traveling so many places and meeting so many people, that's where I began to love God's people black and white. Only white people who would know God's love could love God's people and liberate the slave."

Sarah broke into Richard's storytelling. "And I met your father because of that preaching. I had moved to Philadelphia from Virginia. I met him at the Methodist church. He was mourning the recent death of his first wife, and I got one look at those eyes and knew he was the one for me." She pressed her hand to her husband's chest. "So, in a way, the Lord brought us together with slavery. He was a freed slave and so was I."

"Mom, you were a slave, too?" Sara's mouth dropped.

"That's right, my dear," Richard said as he pulled his wife in for a kiss on the temple.

"Yes, honey. You knew that," Sarah said.

"Well, you need to talk about it more. It makes you more than just Daddy's wife," Sara said.

"Our purposes aligned, and he had asked me to marry him," said Sarah. "I fell in love with his deep and profound faith and his belief in black equality. That belief was exhibited in 1802 when your dad fought the white soldier who was beating a black man. Your dad just whipped him. I knew then he was the one for me. But you're right, Sara. I should testify about it more," she admitted. "I'm not ashamed. The Lord had set me free too. I have been comfortable just serving at the church and helping your dad, but I can add my voice to the struggle." Sarah looked at Richard for his agreement and approval.

He nodded. "Yes, dear. I agree. Yours is a story worth telling, for sure."

"Really, Dad? Is that true? You took on a soldier and won?" James's mouth was agape as he asked the question.

"Yes, son, I couldn't stand by and watch him get killed. I had to put myself in the fray," Richard confessed. "I saw an injustice being committed and knew I needed to interrupt it. I felt a surge of energy come over me, and I got right into his face. In retrospect, I know I could have been severely injured, but for the moment, it didn't matter. I would do it again if need be. I mean right is right, right? Thank God there were other white men in the area who witnessed the beating and who spoke up for me."

"Yes, that was a lesson worthy of the greatest preacher," said his wife.

"And it was solidified in my mind especially after being grabbed multiple times as a runaway slave. I never wanted that hanging over my head again. I was determined to be free—to live free," Richard said. "Slavery is a bitter pill."

"Just walking through the streets of Philadelphia was an exercise in restraint as slaveowners openly defended bondage and everyday Americans debated the concepts of freedom, liberty, and the constitution. Tell them, dear," Sarah said.

"Yes, the debates raged on and still do. And there I am in the middle advocating freedom for the enslaved. And it is on this rock I stand." Richard slapped his thigh. "You know, these songs would make a great addition to the collection of hymns I am compiling. Don't you think so, dear?"

"Oh, yes. It would be great to have these songs regularly sung in churches," Sarah answered.

Richard struck out in song, "*Didn't my Lord deliver Daniel, deliver Daniel, deliver Daniel? Didn't my Lord deliver Daniel, and why not a every man?*" He smiled, then said. "Okay, family, let's go to bed."

Richard blew out the lanterns around the room and the family went to their respective pallets.

Chapter 29

Doxology

In the spring of 1831, an aging Richard Allen lay in his bed surrounded by his children and his wife. He had been ill for several months. Coughing up much phlegm into a handkerchief his wife had handed him, he struggled to get his words out.

"Children, I feel like the Apostle Paul. As I reflect on the life God has given me, I can get what he meant, when he said, 'I have fought a good fight, I have finished my course, I have kept the faith.'"

"Oh Daddy, don't talk like that," Sara, his elder daughter cried out. "It's so negative."

"Don't cry, dear," Ricard tried to comfort her. "I am in my right mind. I have no machinations of my immortality. My time on earth is short."

"Oh, dear heart," Sarah pleaded her cries.

"Hush now. It's just my time. The Scripture states, 'Man that is born of a woman is of few days and full of trouble.' And Good Lord, I have seen my fair share of trouble. I have tried to do some good with my time. Richard Jr., I need you to do something for me," said Allen.

"Yes, Dad, anything."

"I have led an interesting life, wouldn't you agree? Born a slave on Master Chew's farm, then on to Master Sturgis's. I watched my momma sold off and have never seen her again. I found religion when Rev. Freeborn Garretson preached the revival in the woods. I bought my freedom for two thousand colonial dollars. I led the black exodus from St. George's and then started the black church where the white folks tried to rope us back in. They fought us tooth and nail. They even took us to court," Richard sputtered. "But we prevailed. I have stood in the gap fighting slavery and trying to work for black uplift. Your mother and I have hidden fugitive slaves. We've politicked and advocated for black dignity, freedom, and citizenship. I've had the opportunity to eulogize the first President of the United States. I became appointed bishop of the African Methodist Episcopal church, and I've gathered the first national conference for black leaders." Richard spat phlegm into a nearby bucket. "I need to tell the story so that this legacy is not lost."

"Yes, Dad. We need to tell your story. It's a story worth telling," Richard Jr. agreed.

"Will you help me write it?" his father asked. "But first, I need to make sure you all are taken care of. I need to write a will."

"Yes, Father. I'll write it down." Richard Jr. pulled out a pad and prepared to take notes.

"I, Richard Allen, being of sound mind and body, do hereby bequeath the following to my friends and family." Richard recounted his bequests including remembering his children regarding his significant real estate holdings. "For John, I leave this home at 150 Spruce Street. To my married daughters, Sara and Ann and my son, Peter, I leave the parcels on Pine Street and the three-story brick tenement," he continued. "And for my grandchildren Sarah Ann and Richard Nathaniel, I leave two houses and lots on Lombard Street near the church."

"Thank you, Dad," Peter said.

"Take care of it, and it will take care of you, son," Richard said.

Peter wiped a tear from his eye.

"And to my beloved wife, Sarah, I leave several personal rental properties for income for the future. You can sell my home in Hook to pay any remaining debts owed to my executors. The Bethel Church Corporation has ten years to pay only the annual interest it has owed to me," Richard continued weakly. "And to my friend, John Cox, I give a silver-head cane and Burkitt's commentaries on the New Testament. To Joseph Corr, a strong, black preacher, I bequeath six volumes of Josephus's works." He paused, then said, "There, I have recounted all, I think."

Richard Jr. nodded, then turned to another page in the notebook.

"Now we can get on to finalizing my legacy. Children and wife, leave us be, please. Richard Jr., let me tell you what I have thought about over these last few weeks." Looking upward, Richard prayed, "My God, I entered life without acknowledging thee, let me therefore finish it in loving thee."

Richard had three main goals as he delineated his years of service. First, he wanted to tell of the beginnings of the African Methodist Episcopal Church and secondly, the rise of free black people. Finally, he desperately wanted to present to the world a broad view of his story from his humble beginnings to something through hard work, piety, and a firm belief in the American ideals of freedom and justice for all.

Richard told his son, "I have been earnestly solicited by many of my friends to leave a small detail of my life and proceedings."

Richard began his tale, "Mark the perfect man and behold the upright: for the end of that man is peace." He continued, "Son, I wish not to elongate my story as a child of slavery, for truly slavery is a bitter pill. I'd rather fill the pages with tales of black freedom struggles," he said. "Instead, I want to republish some of my earlier tracts: the *Narrative of the Colored People* and our tale of the yellow fever epidemic, and my 1794 antislavery appeal, *Address to the People of Color*. I wish to give, well ... color to the history. I want it to have a very present-day feel. People need to understand that in the gospel of Richard Allen, racial justice would only occur through our black collective struggle," Richard insisted. "Are you getting all this?"

"Yes, Father. 'Collective black struggle,'" his son said.

"And be sure to include the *African Supplement* recalling how we defined black sovereignty in our declaration to be a church despite white claims of ownership. As the courts decided, it was free blacks who built the church, and it would be ours to maintain control of it," Richard said sitting up on his pillow.

Richard went on in detail about the yellow fever epidemic and its impact on the racial justice movement.

"It is important to remember God and a soldier, all men do adore, in time of war, and not before; when the war is over, and all things righted, God is forgotten, and the soldier slighted. In other words, never forget the black bridge that brought you over."

Richard coughed repeatedly.

"And do not forget to publish our articles of faith, hope, and love. In doing so, you will remind future readers 'the Lord has made of one blood all nations.'"

Richard gasped for air as he spoke.

"How would you like this to end?" Richard Jr. asked. "When you have gone the last mile of the way, how would you like the story to be told? I'll tell you how I want you to be remembered. I am not interested in portraying you as some ambivalent race leader, but more of an American freedom fighter who set the stage for radical abolitionism."

"Thank you, son. I'd like to be remembered that way too. Even more so, I'd like for free blacks to remember to be pious and to claim American citizenship as their own," Richard said.

"And what do you have to say to our white allies?"

"I want them to feel our afflictions, to sympathize with us in heart-rending distress, when the husband is separated from the wife, and the parents from the children, who are never more to meet in this world. I want them to know their righteous indignation is roused at the means taken to supply the place of the murdered babe. Continue to blow the trumpet against the mighty evil—make the tyrants tremble." Richard felt another cough coming on. "I simply want them to see and hear the Imago Dei when they encounter their black brethren."

"Ooh, Latin … That's really good, Dad." Richard Jr. scribbled the notes furiously.

"Yes, the Imago Dei. I want my white brothers to see the image of God when they investigate another brown face. Just like I do when I look at yours," Richard reached out to touch his son's face. "I love you, son. I see God in you."

Richard's breathing halted then and his hand slipped from his son's cheek.

"Dad? Daddy!" Richard Jr. shook his father's shoulders, but there was no life left. "Nooooo!" Richard Jr. bent down over his father's bed.

Soon, his mother, sisters and brothers ran into the room responding to his cries.

"Our father is … is no more." He broke into a sob. "He's dead. Our father, the great bishop has preached his own eulogy. Long may his memory be kept alive. May we all remember to live in the image of God." Richard Jr. let himself be bundled into his mother's embrace.

Author's Notes

Bishop Richard Allen (born February 14, 1760) died on March 26, 1831, after a lengthy illness. His corpse is entombed in the basement of Bethel Church where it remains to this day. Sarah Bass Allen (death July 16, 1849) is also interred at Bethel.

Bishop Allen's name is well-known and respected in the Philadelphia area. His name is emblazoned on schools, church buildings, and civic organizations. Sadly, beyond name recognition, there is little known on this incredible man. "Mother Bethel" aims to keep his memory and legacy intact, but his name fades with each generation and his light dims which is partially why I wanted to tell his story.

Bethel is situated in the historical district in South Philadelphia. It is the prime location to remember Bishop Allen. His legacy should be recalled in American history classes and children should be taught about him. Regrettably, his legacy is often hidden/obscured by our minimal black history remembrances. We know the names Reverend Dr. Martin Luther King and Rosa Parks, but while laudatory, their collective work should not discount that of Bishop Allen. He is the progenitor of the American Civil Rights journey. The black exodus from St. George's stands as a pivotal memory of nonviolent social protest. We often talk about the "big six" of the Civil Rights Movement, the men who were the architects of the movement. I submit Bishop Richard Allen, while at least a century separated their work, as a spark igniting the fire.

There has been an ongoing debate regarding whether slavery happened in "the North" and the Richard Allen story refutes that narrative. The truth is slavery was a nationwide problem, in part accepted for its economic benefit to national and personal coffers. Allen, born a slave in Philadelphia, the city of brotherly love, and raised in Delaware, was a renaissance man having impacted thousands with love and commitment—his imprint is still being felt today around the world as AME churches have spread globally.

I am deeply indebted to Reverend James R. Bond, senior pastor of Revival Tabernacle in Watsontown, PA, who supported this work wholeheartedly. I am indebted. Watching him preach these last almost twenty-five years has been inspirational in more ways than one. I hope to preach like you when I grow up.

To Reverend Jeanette Hooks Hubbard, pastor of St. Andrewes AME Church in Youngstown, Ohio, I say thanks for sharing your church's doctrines with me. I didn't know much, but your ministry book was very helpful as I learned about the AME denomination.

I relied heavily upon the work and research of Dr. Richard S. Newman, professor of history at Rochester Institute of Technology who published an authoritative text on Richard Allen titled *Freedom's Prophet: Bishop Richard Allen, the AME Church, and the Black Founding Fathers* (2008) as my source material for this manuscript.

I do want to also thank my critique group, the West Branch Christian Writers (Roberta, Christine, Sue, Nancy, and Jill) who read most of this book. Their constant encouragement was a boon. I would regularly find comments like "This is an important chapter" and "Keep going" and "Good job" on their reviews of my chapters. I often say writing is a solitary endeavor, but it need not be. Everyone needs to find their tribe. I'm glad I found mine.

In 2015, I suffered a stroke after a four-way cardiac bypass.

Typing is difficult, and there were many days I wanted to give up, but thanks to my wife, Darlene Garcia-Johnson, who, in her own way, encouraged me along. Thanks, babe!

To my readers, Kim Rossi, Tenacia Gunn, and Sharon Bond, who read chapters and passages when I got nervous. Your feedback and encouragement were invaluable. Thank you, ladies.

Finally, I wish to extend my deepest gratitude to my editor, Sue A. Fairchild. Your expert advice really shaped the work and made my character's voices louder.

About the Author

Brian C. Johnson honors the struggles and accomplishments of the ordinary citizens who launched the Civil Rights Movement by committing himself personally and professionally to the advancement of multicultural and inclusive education.

He earned both bachelor's and master's degrees in English from California University of Pennsylvania, and a Ph.D. in communications media and instructional technology at Indiana University of Pennsylvania in December 2016. Brian is the co-author of *Reel Diversity: A Teacher's Sourcebook* (2008), winner of the 2009 Phillip Chinn Book Award by the National Association for Multicultural Education and a revised edition in 2015, and *We've Scene It All Before: Using Film Clips in Diversity Awareness Training* (2009). His youth Bible study, *Finding God in the Bathroom*, was published in 2020 and his novel, *God's Not Finished With Me Yet*, followed in 2023.

Brian serves on the ministry team at Revival Tabernacle in Watsontown, Pennsylvania where he is the youth pastor. He is a gifted teacher and enjoys sharing hope and joy with those to whom he ministers.

9 781967 649006